Even and Odd

ALSO BY SARAH BETH DURST

Even and Odd

SARAH BETH DURST

CLARION BOOKS
Houghton Mifflin Harcourt
Boston   New York

Clarion Books

3 Park Avenue

New York, New York 10016

Copyright © 2021 by Sarah Beth Durst

Clarion Books is an imprint of Houghton Mifflin Harcourt Publishing Company.

hmhbooks.com

The text was set in Dante MT.

Library of Congress Cataloging-in-Publication Data is available.

ISBN 978-0-358-35038-5

Manufactured in the United States of America

1 2021

4500825274

To the health care heroes
and all the everyday people
who didn't think they were ready to be heroes
but stepped up anyway

Thank you

'LIKE MANY SISTERS, Even and Odd shared many things:

Their bedroom.

Their closet.

Six pairs of flip-flops.

Use of the living-room TV.

And . . . magic.

On even days, Even could work magic. On odd days, her one-year-younger sister, Odd, could. Years ago, before their family moved across the border from the magic world of Firoth to Stony Haven, the most ordinary town in Connecticut, the sisters had discovered they could each work magic on alternating days. Showing an imperfect understanding of how calendars work, four-year-old Emma had coined their nicknames—and they'd stuck. Emma became Even, and Olivia became Odd.

Now twelve years old, Even wished she'd picked a nickname

that wasn't a constant reminder of the fact that she lacked magic half the time. Like today, which was an odd day.

On odd days, she couldn't practice her magic. If she couldn't practice, she couldn't get better. If she didn't get better, she wouldn't pass all the required levels of Academy of Magic exams and win her wizard medallion. And if she didn't have a medallion, she couldn't become a hero of Firoth, charged with protecting the magic world against all threats—a goal that had been her dream for as long as she could remember.

So, not a fan of odd days.

But at least she was still able to help out with the family's shop on odd days, despite her lack of magic. It helped pass the time until she was magical again. That afternoon, Dad had left her in charge of the register while he went to pick up milk from the supermarket and Odd from her volunteer job at the Stony Haven Animal Rescue Center. Even loved being trusted to help their customers.

Like Frank the centaur, who was here to collect his order.

"So that's one box of nine-by-twelve manila envelopes, one vial of imported ambrosia, and a Three Musketeers bar." Even calculated the cost. "Twenty-six dollars and forty-eight cents. Plus one hundred forty-eight seventy-three for the rare honey shipment. Your total is one hundred seventy-five dollars and twenty-one cents."

Frank handed her his credit card. "Excited about summer vacation? No more teachers, no more books, no more . . . Wait, that's not right. 'No more teachers' dirty looks' is the last one, which means the first one can't be teachers . . ."

She grinned. For as long as he'd been coming into the shop, Frank had liked to try out mundane-world sayings he'd learned. He usually mangled them. "Pencils?" she suggested.

"No more pencils, no more books—yes, that's it! Thanks, Even!"

"Actually, I'm not done with studying yet," Even said. "I take the Academy of Magic level-five exam on Friday. I'm doing the remote course." She'd been studying hard, practicing every even day and poring over her level-five textbook on odd days. She had it all planned out: Once she passed, she'd only have three more levels left until she had her junior-wizard medallion. And once she had *that,* the Academy could start assigning her basic quests in the magic world, like monitoring a phoenix rebirth or helping with a mermaid migration. If she did well enough with *those,* then by the time she was eighteen, she'd have her official—

Frank interrupted her daydream. "Ah, fantastic! Good luck!"

The machine spat out his receipt, and Even handed it to him along with his credit card. "Do you need any help with the honey?" she asked politely.

"Yes—if you could just strap it on my back, that would be great."

Frank was part of a local research team, sponsored by the Academy. He was in the store nearly every other day to pick up special-order items. Currently, his team was studying honey and had ordered samples from across the United States. Last month it had been peanut butter. She hefted the box of honey onto his broad horse's back, and she belted it on with the straps he had for that purpose. He held his other purchases with his human hands.

"Thanks for your business," Even told him, hoping she sounded professional.

"Please tell your parents to call when the next shipment comes in." He clip-clopped to the door. Pausing, he cast an illusion to disguise his horse body as a motorcycle and "rode" outside. She wondered if he knew that his motorcycle didn't spew any exhaust and still kind of made a clip-clop horse sound beneath the engine roar. She waved as the door shut behind him.

That went well, she thought. *One happy customer down. Yay for me.*

Humming to herself, she spent the next few minutes straightening the shop. Built into their family's garage, the shop was crowded with merchandise. Though her parents had renovated both the house and the shop with extra-wide doors to accommodate a variety of visitors, there still wasn't much room for a full-grown centaur to maneuver without bumping into a few shelves. He'd knocked over a display of diapers, sized from pixie to human to troll, as well as a stack of New York City guidebooks.

Their shop carried supplies for the mundane world, as well as imports from the magic world—anything a magical customer might need for their visit here. It was the kind of store known as a border shop. Located in a border town, close to a gateway between worlds, it was where centaurs, fairies, and other overtly magical beings could buy things without needing to shapeshift or pretend they were in costume. It was also the only place where those visiting from Firoth could ask basic questions, such as "What is an airplane, and is it going to eat me?"

The bell rang over the shop door just as Even finished lining up the stacks of *National Geographic*, *Good Housekeeping*, and *People* magazines. Glancing over, she saw that a new customer had come in: a tall, willowy woman wearing an ornately beaded robe that looked as if it belonged at a Renaissance fair. Her pink hair was braided with jewels and gold-coated flowers, showing off her pointy ears.

An elf! A real elf!

"Welcome!" Even said. Her voice squeaked a little. She'd never met an elf before. Usually they stayed in the magic world and weren't interested in anything to do with the mundane world. But here was one, in their shop! She wished Odd were here to see this. Odd wasn't normally interested in much to do with Firoth, but *this* would have impressed her.

Keeping her robe lifted so it wouldn't touch the floor, the elf surveyed the shop and sniffed. "This is serviceable, I suppose. Are you the proprietor?"

"It's my parents' shop, but I can help you. I mean, can I help you?" Even felt as if her tongue were knotted like a pretzel. She tried again. "May I help you with something?" There, that was better.

"Perhaps."

The elf didn't elaborate. Instead she studied the overflowing shelves and counters with an air of faint disapproval. She looked as if she wanted to hold her nose but was too dignified to do so. Even waited, shifting from foot to foot, wondering if she was supposed to make suggestions or ask questions or just wait politely for the customer to decide what she wanted.

At last, the elf pointed one delicate finger toward the highest shelf, directly at a plush animal, a panda that had sat in the shop for so long cobwebs were strung between its ears. "I will purchase that item. It will make a suitable gift."

"Good choice," Even said. "Everyone likes souvenirs. I'm sure whoever—"

"I do not require your approval," the elf interrupted. "I require you to fetch it. I do not wish to expend my magic on a menial task."

"Of course. Sorry." She wasn't exactly sure what she was apologizing for, but there was something about the elf's manner that made Even feel like she'd committed a horrible breach of etiquette. She made a mental note to ask her parents more about the customs of elves. That kind of info wasn't in her theory textbook.

Crossing the shop, she retrieved the ladder and carried it to the shelves. She climbed up to the plush panda and reached toward it.

"Excuse me, *what* are you doing?"

Arm outstretched, Even stopped. "You wanted this one, didn't you?"

"Why are you using such an . . . *ordinary* way to fetch it?"

"I'm not tall enough to reach it without a ladder." She thought that was obvious, but she kept her voice polite. This was a customer, after all.

"This is a border shop, is it not?" the elf demanded.

"It is." Even wasn't sure what the problem was. So far as she knew, she hadn't done anything inappropriate or unprofessional.

"It is supposed to be run by accredited wizards."

"Both of my parents have their wizard medallions," Even

said. Medallions were required to run a shop that carried magical items. According to the laws of Firoth, they were required for any kind of job that involved magic, as well as any sort of official quest, like the kind Even dreamed about, with dragons and unicorns and enchanted stuff. "I'm still a student, but I'm taking my level-five exam soon."

"If you're ready for your level-five, you ought to be able to levitate a simple toy. Have you been so foolish as to let yourself run out of magic?"

Even braced herself, trying not to outwardly cringe. She didn't really want to explain herself to this intimidatingly disapproving customer. "Well, I, um, you see, my sister and I share our magical abilities. I only have magic every other day. And, well, that's not today."

The elf sniffed in disapproval. "Absurd! How can you expect to put in the requisite hours of practice in such a situation? You do not understand the depths of dedication that true wizardry requires."

"I do understand! I work hard!" Even's face felt hot. She stopped reaching for the panda and held on to the ladder.

"Honestly, the presumption of today's youth, to think half an effort is enough—"

"It *is* enough!" The words burst out before Even could stop them—she'd argued this debate with herself before, usually late at night when she couldn't sleep, but she'd *never* had it with a customer. She tried to explain. "I know I'm not ready to be a hero yet, but by the time I'm old enough to get my medallion, I'll be ready for the Academy to grant me a quest—"

"Enough with such foolishness." Frowning, the elf made a gesture with her hands. "If you're truly a hero-to-be, then save yourself from this." Before Even could react, she felt soft, sticky ropes twining around her. She shrieked as she realized it wasn't rope at all—it was spiderweb pulled from the plush panda and grown with magic. The webbing wrapped around her fast, tying her to the ladder.

"What are you doing?" Even cried. "Let me go!"

"I'm teaching you a lesson in humility," the elf said. "It's for your own good. I'll be back to do my shopping when *real* magic users are here." She flicked her hand one more time, and the toy panda flew off the shelf. One leg stuffed itself into Even's mouth so she couldn't yell anymore.

The elf waltzed out the door, with the bell ringing sweetly behind her.

Even spat the panda out. It tumbled to the floor. She ran her tongue around her mouth, spitting out bits of fur and dust. *Blech.* The elf hadn't stuffed the panda in too hard, nor had she tied the webbing too tight. She hadn't been trying to hurt Even, just humiliate her.

Well, she succeeded, Even thought. This ranked up there with the most embarrassing things that had ever happened to her, and that included her near failure on her level-four exam. *Now I'm glad Odd isn't here to see this.*

Squirming, she tried to loosen the cobwebs. The ladder wobbled, but the webbing held tight. The elf had used a lot of it. Even would have been impressed if she weren't the one stuck. She wiggled her fingers, making a space between the threads. Once she got her hands free . . .

For fifteen minutes, she wiggled and squirmed—carefully, so she didn't knock the ladder over. She was sure she'd be able to get out eventually. She just had to be patient. She'd freed her fingers. If she could get up to the elbow, then she could tear the rest off . . .

Outside, she heard a car pull into the driveway. *Oh no.* She wiggled and squirmed faster. She'd just gotten her left arm out up to the elbow when Odd came through the back door to the shop, the one that connected the supply closet with the laundry room of their house. For a brief instant, Even wished the webbing had cocooned her completely to spare her the humiliation.

"So I had the worst, most embarrassing, most horrible day—" Odd halted, staring, and then rushed over to the ladder. "Even! Are you okay? Are you hurt?"

"Hey, Odd, everything's fine," Even said casually. She could feel her cheeks blushing bright red again. *This is so not my day,* she thought. "How was the shelter? You were saying you had a bad day?"

Still gawking up at her, Odd said, "Um, yeah, my magic malfunctioned, and I accidentally levitated a labradoodle puppy. One of the other volunteers saw and thought I was trying to throw it. It was a nightmare. I was so scared they were going to kick me out, but they decided it was a misunderstanding—why are you tied to the ladder with cobwebs? Are you sure you're okay?"

"Sure, all good," Even said. She paused, and then: "I could maybe use a little help getting down," she admitted.

Odd began to pull the webbing off her.

"Quickly, before Mom or Dad comes in. Can't you use magic?"

Climbing up the first couple of rungs, Odd continued to claw the strands away. Loose cobweb stuck to her arms and hair. "Mom's on a magic-mirror call, and Dad's putting away the groceries. Trust me, my way will be faster. What happened?"

"It wasn't my fault. It was a customer. She was upset that I didn't have magic." Even couldn't help it—her voice wobbled as she spoke. *Why couldn't we have been born with normal magic?* She'd never heard of anyone else with split magic. It wasn't fair.

"You told her it wasn't your day, right? Explained about the calendar thing?"

"I told her we alternate days. She did not like that. But it's fine. I'm going to ace my exam, and then she'll be eating her words." If Even said it with enough conviction, maybe she could squelch that nasty bit of self-doubt that kept whispering: *What if I'm not good enough? What if no matter how hard I work, I'm never good enough?* Usually it was easy to push the doubt down, but the elf had brought it all back up anew.

"You *are* going to ace it." Odd finished pulling the threads off Even's left leg. "You've certainly been practicing enough this time around. It won't be like level four."

Hearing Odd say that *did* help. It was nice that her sister believed in her. *It doesn't matter what a stranger thinks,* Even told herself. *All that matters is what I choose to do.* She wished she could make herself fully believe that. "You know, you could practice with me. Well, not the same day as me, obviously, but we could both practice! Remember the first time you turned me into a skunk?"

"Yeah, you were being annoying."

"You turned me into a half skunk, half cat, but then you practiced—"

"Because you kept being annoying. And because it was funny."

"—and you got better at it. If you practiced other kinds of magic, not just skunking me—"

Clearing away the last of the cobwebs from Even's arms and

legs, Odd shrugged. "No, thanks. You know I don't want to be a wizard. Magic's just not my thing."

Even plucked a clump of cobweb out of her hair. "I'm not saying you have to be a wizard if you don't want to. You can be my sidekick."

"Seriously?"

"Yes, seriously." Even climbed down the ladder and began gathering up clumps of web. Sticky, they clung to her. "Wait, you meant that sarcastically. I'm being serious! You don't have to do magic, but you can still come with me on my adventures when we're both old enough."

Peeling the sticky cobwebs away, they shoved them into the trash can. "What makes you so sure I'd be your sidekick?" Odd asked. "Maybe you'll be *my* sidekick. You can clean out the litter boxes in the animal shelter while I cuddle the kittens."

Even pretended she didn't hear her. Keeping an absolutely straight face, she said, "I could transform you into a cat. Or how about a hamster? I'll be a wizard of the realm, and you'll be my adorable talking-animal sidekick!"

"You'd better not still be serious."

After disposing of the last of the webbing, Even patted Odd on the shoulder. "Don't worry. I still have years more of training before I'm even close to being a hero. You'll have lots of time to get used to being a talking hamster."

Odd picked the plush panda off the floor and brandished it like a sword.

Even laughed as Odd chased her around the shop with the panda.

THE NEXT MORNING, Monday, an even day, Even sprang out of bed. Concentrating, she floated upward until she touched the ceiling. She pushed herself down, bounced off her bed at an angle, and flew to a wall. Like an astronaut in zero gravity, she shoved against it and sailed across to the opposite side of the room.

Below her, still tangled in covers, Odd opened one eye. "Seriously?"

"Sorry!" Even sang as she propelled herself off another wall, crumpling the edge of a poster. *Not perfect,* she thought. She'd have to work on that. She wanted to be flawless on the exam so there would be no question that she was ready for the next level of training. The level-four exam had been way too close a call—she'd squeaked by, passing by only a few points, thanks to a solid shapeshift into a chicken and no thanks to a disastrous levitation attempt that had resulted in mayonnaise everywhere. The level-five exam would be even harder.

"It's seven-fifteen." Odd pulled her blanket over her head. "And I hate you."

"You hate mornings," Even corrected.

Muffled, Odd moaned, "It's summer vacation!"

"It's an even day." Even was fine with sleeping as late as Odd wanted on odd days, but she wasn't about to waste a second of an even day. Especially one so close to an Academy exam. She only had today and Wednesday to finish preparing.

Other magic students didn't have to wait through magicless days. They could practice whenever they wanted. But she wasn't going to squander today wallowing in self-pity about what she didn't have. If Even only had half her life with magic, then she was just going to work twice as hard.

Plus, flying was awesome.

She launched herself across the room again and studied the distance to the door. If she aimed right, she thought she might be able to propel herself out of the bedroom and into the bathroom in one move. *One, two, three . . .* She kicked off and flew across the room, through the doorway, across the hall, and into the bathroom.

Crash.

She hit the shower curtain, and the curtain rod clattered

into the bathtub. It sounded like metal scaffolding collapsing. Even landed on top of it in the tub. A shampoo bottle toppled into her lap. "I'm fine!" she shouted quickly.

That hadn't exactly gone as she'd pictured, but, she consoled herself, she still had time to perfect her turns. Besides, flying an obstacle course wasn't required until level seven. *It's going to be okay,* she told herself. *I'm ready.*

Or at least I will be ready.

She just needed a little more practice before Friday.

Mom called up the stairs, "Everything okay?"

"I said I'm fine!"

"Any broken bones?"

"All fine!" Untangling herself from the curtain, Even climbed out of the tub. She knocked a bottle of conditioner and a bar of soap onto the floor.

"Any bleeding?"

"Completely fine!"

Wrestling with the curtain rod, Even lifted it over her head. On tiptoes, she raised it as high as she could, wedging it into position. Stepping back, she examined it. It was slightly lopsided. With magic, she tried to shift the left side up to straighten it. It rose six inches, the other side lost its grip, and the curtain clattered again into the bathtub.

"Still fine!" she called.

Odd shuffled into the bathroom. Together they lifted the rod back into position, and Even put away all the shampoo bottles and soaps she'd knocked off. "Thanks," she said to her sister.

"Summer *vacation*," Odd repeated.

"The exam is this Friday!" If Even didn't pass, she would not be eligible to take it again for another year . . . and next year the test was scheduled for an odd day. She didn't know about the year after that, but two years was already too long to wait. If she wanted her medallion by the time she was a grownup, she had to stay on schedule.

Odd sighed dramatically and rolled her eyes, but she stopped arguing.

If Odd had been trying for her medallion, she'd have been anxious to practice as much as possible too. Not for the first time, Even wondered why they wanted such different things. They'd been raised together — same parents, same house, same school. *Sometimes I don't understand her at all.*

"If I were to transform into a penguin, would it cheer you up?" Even offered. She still needed to practice her transformations. That was a key part of level five. She'd have to achieve five transformations within fifteen minutes, without running out of magic.

"No."

"Baby buffalo?"

"No."

"Chinchilla? Everyone loves a chinchilla. Softest rodent ever. Densest fur of all land animals. Second only to the sea otter, if you count land *and* sea."

Another of Odd's spectacular eye rolls. "You could let me have first shower."

"Deal." Even scooted out into the hallway, and Odd shut the door. While the water ran, Even considered chinchilla versus penguin, and decided a penguin would be a better choice. She knew of multiple kinds of penguins—Adélie, macaroni, rockhopper, Galápagos, African—but her favorite was the largest, the emperor penguin.

She pictured it: three and a half feet tall, white belly, black head and flippers, pale yellow neck, bright yellow ear patches. Carefully, she squeezed her image of herself inside the penguin. Beginning the transformation, she stuffed her hair beneath smooth black feathers, stretched her nose into a beak that narrowed into a tip, smoothed and flattened her arms into flippers . . .

Out of the corner of her eye, she saw her mom start up the stairs with a basket of laundry, and Even's focus began to slip, now that she knew she had an audience.

"Stiffen your tailfeathers," Mom advised as she passed the bathroom. "Fourteen to eighteen feathers in a wedge shape."

"Thanks," Even squawked through her penguin beak. She refined her tailfeathers.

From within the shower, Odd called, "Mom, don't encourage her!"

"You were supposed to be surprised!" Even called back to Odd.

"For me to be surprised, you'd need to not be predictable!"

Finishing the transformation, Even admired her penguin self. She'd done a particularly fine job on the webbed feet. Not that Odd would appreciate it. *Oh well,* Even thought. *I'm not doing this for her.*

Or with her.

Even waddled into her parents' bedroom as she transformed herself back into a human girl. Her parents' bedroom was Even's favorite place in their house. It had all the usual furniture you'd expect: bed, dresser, mirror, bedside tables—but each piece came with a special twist. The bed lay beneath a lace canopy interwoven with fairy-made lights that danced while you slept, the dresser was a gift from a mermaid family and covered in shells that crooned love songs, the mirror was enchanted to tell you news reports from across the border, and the tables could summon any book from any shelf in the house. All the other rooms in their house had to be practical, because you couldn't predict who would visit, but the master bedroom was allowed to be extraordinary.

Usually the sight of her parents' room made her smile. But today Mom's suitcase lay open on the bed, beneath the twinkling canopy. Seeing the suitcase, Even felt the last of her good mood dribble away. She'd forgotten that Mom was leaving for another business trip this morning. Another trip to Firoth without Even.

Mom was pairing socks from the laundry basket while blouses marched over her head from the closet to her suitcase, folding themselves in midair. She was wearing a similar blouse with suit pants, her hair was pinned into a bun, and she'd applied her trademark plum lipstick—her suburban professional costume, she called it. She glanced at Even. "Missed a flipper."

Glancing down at her body, Even saw she had one human arm and one penguin flipper. Concentrating, she rounded and stretched the flipper back into its usual shape. She wiggled her fingers to test them. "You know, if you took me with you to Firoth, I think it would be very beneficial for my magical education."

"Nice try," Mom said. "I told you: when you're older."

"When I'm a grownup and have my medallion, I won't need your permission to go," Even pointed out. "It'll be my job to protect the magic world as a hero of the realm."

Mom's mouth twitched as if she wanted to smile but didn't want Even to see. "But that time isn't now. You have a whole lifetime to have adventures. Enjoy relaxing at home while you can."

"I'll be perfectly behaved if you let me come," Even said. "Quiet as a mouse." She had an idea. "I could transform into a mouse and travel in your pocket! Or a chipmunk, if you don't like mice. No one will know I'm there."

"I'll know."

"Will it help if I beg?"

Mom stopped folding socks, and the blouses halted in mid-air. "Even."

"Okay, that's a no." It was impressive how parents could fill a name with entire unspoken sentences. For example, when Mom said, "Even," she was really saying, *You have asked me three thousand four hundred ninety-seven times, and the answer is no,* non, nein, nyet, *and nope in as many languages as I can think of.* "You'll still be back in time for my exam, right?"

"Of course. It's my usual trip." Mom would be traveling to various towns and cities to spread word of their border shop and drum up more customers. Lots of meetings crammed into just a few days. She went a couple of times a year, and it always led to more new business for them. "I'll be home on Thursday, in time to help you with any last-minute studying, if you'd like. In the meantime, I expect you to help your dad with the shop."

Outside, footsteps paused in the hallway, and Odd stuck her head in. She was dressed in her usual black T-shirt, black-rimmed glasses, and jean shorts, but she hadn't bothered to dry her hair. Her wet hair had dampened the shoulders of her shirt. "You're going again?"

"As soon as I'm packed." After counting her shirts, Mom

sent one floating back into the closet. It draped itself over a hanger.

"Do you have to?" Odd asked. "I hate it when you go away. What if something happens to you while you're gone? Or to us and you're not here?" For as long as Even could remember, Odd had never liked it when Mom went on business trips.

Mom sighed. "Odd."

This time, Even thought Mom was really saying, *It's not healthy to think of the worst-case scenario all the time, especially in situations that are out of your control.* She'd said that to them often enough.

"I know," Odd said. "Deep breath, and count five things I'm grateful for." She plopped down on the bed next to Even. Her hair dripped on the bedspread. "I'd be a lot more grateful if you didn't have to go."

Mom closed her suitcase. "It's just a short trip. Everything is going to be fine."

Odd clapped her hands over her ears. "You're going to jinx us!"

"Even, tell your sister she's being ridiculous," Mom said. "I have to go."

Even leaned closer. "You're being ridiculous. She has to go."

Odd lowered her hands.

"Odd, tell your sister she's being ridiculous," Mom said. "She can't come."

"You asked again?"

"I always ask," Even said.

"Exactly. And she always says no."

"Someday she will say yes." Even had to believe that. This mundane world might be home, but Firoth was her future!

"Experience says otherwise."

"Optimism is a life choice," Even said loftily.

Mom picked up her suitcase and smiled at them both. She then frowned at Odd and flicked her free hand at Odd's head. A trickle of water arched from her hair, across the bedroom, and into Mom's bathroom sink. In seconds, Odd's hair was dry.

"I wish I could do that," Even said with a sigh. Mom made it look so easy! Of course, she'd been able to practice every day for decades.

"Do your chores, go to bed on time, and don't make your father's life more difficult. Even, that means no bothering your father with a million questions about magic. Odd, that means helping in the shop even if you don't feel like it."

"Yes, Mom!" they chorused.

The sisters trailed after her, out of the bedroom, down the stairs, and into the kitchen. Even floated a few inches off the floor at all times. *Look, Mom,* she thought. *I can do magic and mope at the same time. Is that on the exam?*

"Even, watch your magic usage."

Even dropped to the floor. She still had plenty left for today

—she could feel it tingling just under her skin—but Mom was right that it was important to be aware. Magic worked like a phone battery. You could only use a certain amount before you needed to rest and let yourself recharge. "I need to practice."

"Don't overdo it. It won't be the end of the world if you don't pass on your first try." Mom twitched her fingers, and a granola bar flew into her purse for breakfast. Even was certain that Mom hadn't needed multiple attempts to pass any of her exams. Nor had Dad. Or anyone they knew.

"I know, Mom."

"I'm serious, Even. This test is not a measure of what kind of person you are; it's just a measure of how well you take tests. In the grand scheme of things, it's not that important."

It's important to me, Even thought. But she didn't say it out loud. She knew Mom was just trying to make her feel better. Still . . . a part of her couldn't help but think that it sounded a little like Mom didn't believe she was good enough to do it. And that little part couldn't help but wonder if Mom was right. Even squashed self-doubt down as hard as she could. Trying to sound one hundred percent confident, she declared, "I'll pass all my level exams, win my medallion, and then do great things."

"You can do plenty of great things right now," Mom said. "Like cleaning your room. And doing your laundry. I don't want to come home and find you're re-wearing socks."

"Mom! There is absolutely nothing heroic about laundry."

Laughing, Mom hugged Even and Odd. "I'll be back soon," she promised them. "Don't worry. Your dad will be here the entire time."

They followed her to the door and then watched her through the kitchen window.

If they'd lived in the magic world, Mom might have flown or transformed into a bird or ridden a flying horse, but here, she simply got into her car to drive to the gateway between worlds, which was hidden behind the bagel shop.

As Mom pulled out of the driveway, Even wished again she could run after her and go with her. *When I'm old enough and ready, I'll be able to live my dream*, she promised herself.

She wished she were ready now.

3

"I'M GOING TO make breakfast!" Even announced. It was the perfect task: she'd get to practice her magic, and they'd both be cheered up by yummy food.

Odd winced. "Please don't. Remember last time?"

Last time had resulted in scrambled eggs in her hair. Also on the ceiling. But that was last time. She'd practiced a lot of levitation since then. "Practice makes perfect!"

Odd applauded sarcastically. "Very inspirational and original. But, counterpoint: last time, there were half-cooked eggs in my shoes, which were in the living room. So I'm thinking perfection may be a long way off."

"No scrambled eggs this time," Even said. "Pancakes."

"I want yogurt."

Even raised her eyebrows at Odd. *Hello, bad mood.* Yes, it was never fun when Mom left for another of her business trips, but there was no reason for Odd to aim her grumpiness at her sister.

All Even wanted was to practice her magic, have a nice break-fast, and forget about yesterday's mess with the elf and how it had made her feel. "No one *wants* yogurt. People only eat it to make themselves feel like they're being healthy." She focused on a cabinet, and it opened. Carefully, she lifted a bowl into the air with her mind. It wobbled.

"I happen to like it." Crossing to the fridge, Odd picked out a container of yogurt and scowled at it. "Except blueberry. It's like half goop. Okay, fine, let's do pancakes. But I'm cooking them with you this time."

"Good sidekick practice," Even said approvingly.

Odd glared at her.

Even grinned back.

Letting the bowl settle on the table, Even took advantage of the open fridge to send ingredients flying: two eggs and a stick of butter. She was bracing herself to lift the milk when Odd plucked it out of the fridge and carried it to the counter.

"I had it!" Even protested.

Ignoring her, Odd set the griddle on the stove.

Quickly, before Odd could turn it on, Even focused on the dial and twisted it to medium. She slid open the drawer with the measuring cups and lifted them out. Opened the bag of flour. Scooped out a cup. Concentrating, she flew it to the bowl and dumped it in. Flour poofed into the air in a cloud of white dust. She added another half cup, pouring it more care-fully this time.

Odd melted the butter in the microwave while Even flew an egg to the edge of the bowl. She lowered it against the edge. She hadn't hit it hard enough to crack. Squeezing her hands into fists, she aimed again and tried to bring the egg down harder but not too hard.

It tapped the edge of the bowl.

"Let me—" Odd began.

Concentrating, Even tried again, but this time the egg came down too hard. It crashed against the bowl, and the shell shattered. Egg goo spattered. It dripped over the lip of the counter. Rushing forward, Even grabbed a paper towel and wiped it off.

Glaring hard, Odd held out a strand of hair with egg goo clinging to it.

"Sorry," Even said.

"I don't understand why you insist on doing this by magic," Odd complained as she rinsed her hair in the sink. "It doesn't taste better because the ingredients were levitated, and it's a million times easier if you use your hands. Some things are *better* done without magic."

Stepping back, Even locked her hands behind her back and used magic to stir the batter with a spoon. Carefully, she lifted a scoop of batter and poured it onto the hot griddle. It sizzled as it spread into a circle. "If you don't understand, I can't explain it to you."

Odd rolled her eyes. "Seriously? That's not even remotely an answer. And don't try to tell me that becoming a hero has anything to do with making a magical pancake."

"It's practice!"

"You can't claim it's because your stupid test is Friday. You do this every other day—"

"I'd do it every day, if I could." Why was Odd acting like this? She *knew* Even liked to do as much magic as possible on even days. And why was she calling the exam "stupid"? It was the Academy of Magic's official exam! The Academy was in charge of regulating all magical endeavors in Firoth. Once you had their approval—

"There's nothing wrong with doing things the normal way." To emphasize this, Odd took plates out of the cabinet and laid them on the table. "See? Easy."

Hands still behind her back, Even guided the spatula under the pancake as it bubbled. "But it's not as awesome," she said as she flipped the pancake over. As soon as it finished cooking, she sent the pancake flying across the kitchen to land on a plate.

It skidded off the plate and slid onto the floor.

Even and Odd stared at it for a moment.

"That one's yours," Odd said.

Even continued making pancakes and flying them through the air until there were three on each plate, including a plate for Dad. Batter was spattered across the stovetop and counter. *But none on the ceiling!* she thought, pleased with herself. *See, that's progress.* "I don't understand why you're acting like you're anti-magic," she said. "It's a part of you. Of us."

"I'm not anti-magic!" Odd said. "It's just . . . there's a time and a place for it. Sometimes it just makes things worse. Like at school. And in the animal shelter."

Suddenly, Even understood. This wasn't about Mom's business trip or about Even's breakfast failures. "You're upset about yesterday at the shelter."

Odd slumped in her chair. "I told Mom and Dad about it, and they said I shouldn't volunteer at the shelter on odd days until I have my magic under better control—I get too excited around animals. They said I'm just not ready yet."

"You can still go on even days," Even said, trying to cheer her up.

Scowling, Odd drowned her pancakes in maple syrup. "There are supposed to be new kittens coming tomorrow. Kittens! And I can't go help."

Even tried to think of something that would make things better. "How about we do something fun together tomorrow, on your day? Get your mind off the kittens and the puppies. We could—"

Before she finished, Dad waltzed into the kitchen. "Ah, girls! You're awake! Wonderful!" He spun around them, pausing only to plop a kiss on each of their heads. "And pancakes! Yum! Going to have to eat quick, though—we have an item coming in for un-cursing!"

"Yes!" Even jumped up. Un-cursings were her favorite. Dad always let them help. He said it added to the production if his kids were involved, and the bigger the fuss, the happier the customer.

Dad always wanted everyone to be as happy as he was. According to him, he'd been born in a berry patch at the base of a rainbow during a festival of flower fairies, and that accounted for his naturally cheerful personality. Also for his hair. Even wasn't sure there was any truth to that story, but it was true that both his hair and his beard were rainbow-striped. He told everyone it was dyed, but it was natural. Even had blue streaks in her hair, inherited from him, and Odd's natural hair was lavender, though she dyed it black.

Picking up a pancake with his fingers, Dad ate it forkless. "Don't tell your mother," he said, winking at them as he waved the pancake in the air to show that that was what he was talking about. "Delicious. You'll need to get dressed first, Even. Hurry, though. The customer will be here any minute. Just got word from Mr. Fratelli that she's on her way." Carrying his second and third pancakes, he scooted back out of the kitchen.

Even shoveled a few more bites of her pancake into her mouth, and then she concentrated on her clothes. Imagining shorts and a T-shirt, she morphed her PJs into them.

"Ew," Odd said.

"What?" Even checked herself. She'd remembered the front and back of her shirt and shorts. She retrieved her sneakers from beside the door and put them on.

"That doesn't substitute for showering."

"It's fine."

"You're going to smell."

Even was *not* going to miss an un-cursing because of her younger sister's obsession with cleanliness. Her skin wouldn't flake off if she skipped one shower. "You know, in the old days, people bathed once a month."

"And died at, like, age thirty-two."

"I'm not going to die if I don't shower for one day."

"But you'll stink."

Holding an image in her mind, Even concentrated. She felt her body shrink as the kitchen zoomed up around her. A tail sprouted behind her. Fur burst out over her skin, black and shiny except for one white stripe.

As a skunk, Even pranced around the kitchen. "How about this? Do I smell better now?" Stopping in front of Odd, she did a handstand, stuck her rear in the air, and wiggled her tail.

Odd laughed and then rolled her eyes. "Real mature, Even.

Tell me again which of us is older? Oh yes, it's you. Even if we count in rodent years."

"Technically, skunks aren't rodents. I am a magnificent mephitid!" With her lovely fluffy tail held high, Even trotted through the laundry room to the back door of the shop. She was proud she'd remembered the word "mephitid" from her animal books.

Set far enough apart to nearly fit a centaur, the shelves felt like a canyon to a skunk. But these canyon walls were overflowing with hair gel, superglue, seltzer, nail polish, honey-wheat pretzels, ziplock bags, baby wipes, googly eyes, and Miracle-Gro plant food—every mundane item currently in demand in the magic world.

Behind her, Odd said, "You'd better change back before Dad sees you and freaks out. Or before he makes me take you to the shelter."

"Dad likes when I use my magic."

"He won't like a skunk in the shop, especially with a customer coming."

Even knew that, but she loved showing off her magic to Dad. She was certain without even looking at the mirror that she'd shifted into a very realistic skunk. She'd been studying her National Geographic animal encyclopedia all year. *He's going to be impressed,* she thought. *I need someone to be impressed with me.* Between the embarrassing incident with the elf and Mom's speech about not needing to pass the test . . . she needed a boost. "I'll change before any customer sees me," she promised.

"He'll think I did it," Odd warned.

Changing Even into a skunk was Odd's specialty, at least when she was annoyed with her sister. She usually skunked Even at least once a year. "Dad knows it's an even day." That was why she thought Dad would be impressed—Even had never changed herself into a skunk before.

She poked her skunk nose around the corner of a shelf. The shop was decorated with thousands of Christmas tree lights wrapped around every shelf and threaded through the rafters in the ceiling. Disco balls in the corners multiplied the lights. Even liked to pretend she was stepping into a meadow lit by fairy lights when she walked into the store.

"Hey, Dad, we're here for the un-cursing."

Dad turned and spotted her. "Even! Why are you a— Did Odd— No, of course not, it's an even day. This is all you. Fantastic transformation! What a tail! You've clearly been practicing. Well done."

"Thanks!" She knew she could count on Dad to give her exactly the reaction she wanted. He was an excellent cheerleader. *I am good at this.* Very pleased, Even focused on her own image and imagined her skunk self stretching, shedding its fur . . .

Weirdly, nothing happened. She stayed a skunk.

"Beautiful job from tip to tail," he said, still admiring her skunkiness. "Odd, can you help me set up the cauldron while your sister shapeshifts back into herself?"

Odd stepped over her and threaded between counters to reach the cauldron, which was balanced on top of a stack of books about Hollywood, the moon landing, the history of chocolate, and other human achievements.

Even took a few deep breaths to steady her thoughts. Concentrating, she pictured herself: an inch taller than Odd, blue-and-black hair, two scrawny human arms and legs, a mosquito bite on her left elbow. She imagined inserting a skunk into that shape . . .

Odd set the cauldron down with a *thump* next to the cash register.

Exhaling, Even examined herself. Still one hundred percent skunk. She hadn't felt so much as a tingle.

Trying not to worry, Even shook herself, shedding fur. Maybe she was overthinking it. Or maybe she was overtired. Or out of magic, though how could that be? It was still early in the day. She shouldn't be anywhere near her limit. Where was the usual tingle?

"Even, aren't you going to change?" Dad asked.

She opened her mouth to ask Dad if he knew what she was doing wrong, but stopped herself. She didn't want him thinking she wasn't ready for the exam. Asking how to transform back into her usual shape was *definitely* the kind of question that might make him think she wasn't ready. "One minute."

"You're not going to be able to help if you don't have opposable thumbs," he cautioned. "You'll miss the un-cursing." As he spread a black velvet tablecloth over the counter, Odd helped fetch supplies from shelves and line them up next to the cauldron: a quart of water purified by a unicorn, dirt from a dragon mountain, holly leaves (labeled WINGS OF BAT), and a can of Sprite that had been wrapped in paper labeled with runes to look more magical.

"Come on, Even, change," Odd said. "You're the one who should be doing this, not me. This is your thing."

Closing her eyes, Even tried a third time. Again, nothing happened. *What's wrong with me?* she wondered. She'd never had trouble with this before.

The bell rang over the shop door.

And the elf who had trapped her in cobwebs walked in.

Even froze. *Oh no, I can't be a skunk in front of her!* It had been humiliating when the elf thought Even wasn't magical enough, but to now be caught with her magic failing to work right . . .

That would be beyond mortifying. Gritting her sharp teeth, she concentrated so hard that her fur vibrated.

She exhaled, panting. Still a skunk.

Dad bowed to the customer. "High Priestess, welcome to our humble border store!"

Oh great, Even thought. *She's not just an elf. She's an* important *elf, witnessing my failure. How fun.*

"Indeed it is that." The elf priestess sniffed. "You are the owner?"

"My wife and I run the shop together," Dad said. "And these are my daughters. It's a family business." He gestured to Odd and Even. His eyes widened as he saw that Even still looked the same. He managed to keep his smile plastered in place.

Even tried a shrug, but it was lost in the fluffiness of her skunk fur.

"Unusual offspring," the elf said.

"My eldest is typically not so furry," Dad said with a forced laugh.

Even wished she could hide as the elf fixed her with a pointed look. But then the elf seemed to dismiss her as inconsequential. Crossing the shop, she withdrew a gold-embroidered pouch from the folds of her voluminous robe, opened it, and lifted out an amulet on a heavy gold chain. She was careful to touch only the chain. Spinning, the amulet glittered in the shop's Christmas lights. "You will assist with this."

Dad nodded. "Cursed?"

"Thrice cursed."

Even wanted to ask what that meant. How could something be thrice cursed? Three different curses? Or cursed three different times so it was three times as powerful? And what kind of curse was it? Death? Sleep? *Permanent skunk shape?* she wondered. *Am I cursed?*

Obviously not. She couldn't be cursed, since she'd transformed herself. She was just having a little difficulty with her focus. Once the elf left, she was sure she'd be able to concentrate again. It was the presence of the high priestess that was throwing her off her game. She hadn't liked being wrapped in cobwebs. *Yes, that must be it.*

"Odd, the ingredients please," Dad said.

Odd shot a look at Even but obeyed Dad without a word. She poured the unicorn water into the cauldron and then added the dragon dirt, plus a few ordinary Mentos to add extra fizz.

To the elf, Dad said, "You may wish to stand back. We will be creating a potent anti-magic potion. You might not like the sensation of being splashed by it." That was pure showmanship. Even knew from experience that it wouldn't do anything if it splashed her. It only affected magical items.

The elf closed her robe and stepped backwards against a counter piled with comic books, trading cards, and collectible action figures. "What assurances can you give me that this will work?"

"Every assurance," Dad said cheerfully. "It's never failed."

Odd crumpled up the dried holly leaves. Even wished she were helping. She usually did it with a lot more flair than Odd. You had to make a show of it!

"I will require proof," the elf said.

Dad held up a hand. "Shh! This is the sensitive part."

With another look at Even, Odd held up the can of Sprite and pulled the tab.

The elf tensed as Odd poured the soda into the cauldron. It bubbled and fizzed as it hit the Mentos. Eyes glued to the cauldron, Dad beckoned to the elf. "Lower the cursed item into the brew."

Carrying the amulet by the chain, the elf came forward.

Everyone held their breath.

Releasing the chain, the elf dropped the amulet. It landed in the soda concoction with a *plop*, and the elf jumped backwards to avoid the splash.

"You have prepared the mixture correctly?" the elf demanded.

"Absolutely," Dad said.

In truth, only one ingredient was necessary. It was the soda that did the trick. Soda negated magic. Not that it was super powerful—it didn't affect magical beings—but it did an excellent job on stuff like cursed amulets, enchanted roses, and unco-operative spell books. They only mixed in all the other junk because Dad insisted that no one from the magic world would believe a non-magic substance could be effective on its own. Plus he liked the theatrics.

I'm supposed to be helping, Even thought. She was the one who loved this, not Odd. She was the sister who liked all things magical.

They waited for a minute with Dad holding up his hand for silence.

Dad reached into the cauldron and pulled out the amulet with a flourish. "All done!"

The elf stayed motionless, halfway across the shop. "I said I wanted proof. If you are so certain that it is safe, then give it to one of your daughters. Preferably the daughter who is not so frivolous as to greet customers as a rodent."

"Technically, a skunk is not a—" Even began.

Odd nudged Even's stomach with her foot, and Even fell quiet.

Dad handed the amulet to Odd by the chain. Twisting the pendant in the twinkling lights, Odd studied it for a moment. Rising up onto her hind feet, Even tried to get a look at it. It was your standard magic amulet: ornate metal twisted around some kind of giant jewel, in this case a big, tacky yellow stone.

"What's the curse supposed to do?" Odd asked.

"Makes your skin turn to scales, your hair fall from your head, your teeth blacken, and your blood boil," the elf said. "My enemy wished for me to suffer an ugly death."

Even rubbed up against Odd's ankles. "Let me do it. I can do this!" She knew Odd would far rather play with puppies than with magical artifacts that could potentially cause death. Of course, there wasn't really any danger. Dad would never have involved them if there had been. But it was supposed to be Even's job as a future hero to take such risks.

"It must be tested on a being similar to me," the elf said.

But I'm more like you! Even thought. *It's my magic day!* Except that her magic wasn't working. Maybe the elf was right.

"Proceed," the elf said.

Odd closed her hand over the jewel.

And nothing happened.

No scales. No blackened teeth. No boiled blood. She was exactly herself. Only Even noticed that her other hand was trembling slightly.

The elf's description of the curse scared her, Even thought, *and I couldn't help because I'm a stupid skunk.* Concentrating, she tried again to transform, but she didn't even feel the slightest tickle. *What's wrong with me?*

Satisfied with her proof, the elf paid Dad for the un-cursing, as well as for the plush panda she'd wanted the day before, and then swept out of the store. A faint smell of roses followed her.

"Thank you for your help, Odd," Dad said when she'd left. "Even, I'm surprised you didn't want to participate. I thought you enjoyed these appointments." His disappointment in her made Even want to cry — she'd *wanted* to be a part of it! He didn't wait for her to explain, though. He scooped up the cauldron and carted it into the house to clean it in the sink.

Even and Odd were left alone in the shop.

"I feel ridiculous every time I do that," Odd complained. "Why didn't you change back?" She put away the ingredients, tossing the soda can into a recycling bin and closing the jars of herbs.

"Sorry," Even said miserably.

"It wasn't even funny when you first transformed. It's *really* not funny now. Who were you trying to impress? Dad? The elf?"

Sprawling on the floor, Even rested her chin on the tile. "Really sorry."

Odd stopped cleaning. "Even, is everything okay?"

Even wanted to say, *Yes, of course, everything's great! It's an even day!* Everything was always great on an even day, and if it wasn't, then magic could always cheer her up. But she couldn't say that. In a very small voice, Even said, "I can't do it."

Squatting next to her, Odd asked, "What did you say?"

"I can't change back," Even whispered.

"What?"

"I'm stuck. Like this. I'm stuck as a skunk."

4

'EVEN WAS CERTAIN she'd be human again by morning. After all, she'd never had any of her magic last into an odd day. Curled up on her bed with her nose resting on her fluffy tail, she told herself this over and over until she finally fell asleep.

She dreamed she was riding her bike down the bike path, on the way to buy bagels from the bagel store. And she woke feeling as if she'd been pedaling. She stretched out her arms, legs, and tail—

Tail?

Seeing the black-and-white fur, she jumped to her four paws with her tail stiff and straight up. A puff of wet air spurted out—

Odd sat bolt upright in bed. "Ahh! What is that smell?"

"Look at me!" Even wailed.

Jumping up, Odd clamped her hands over her nose and mouth. "Don't have to. I can smell you." Backing toward the bedroom door, she said, "We have to tell Dad. This has gone on way too long."

Yesterday they'd told him Even was practicing staying in the same shape for as long as possible, and he'd been happy to hear that. It was a nicely plausible explanation for why she hadn't helped with the un-cursing. Almost an admirable one.

"Mom said not to bother him." *And I don't want him to say I'm not ready for the level-five exam,* Even thought. It was bad enough that she kept thinking it.

I have to be ready! If she missed it, it could be years before the exam date fell on an even day again. Worse, not taking it would feel like saying she wasn't as good as kids her age who had magic every day. *Maybe even like saying I'll* never *be as good as them,* she thought. It would be admitting that the little voice of doubt that nagged at her was right, that practicing every other day wasn't ever going to be enough, and she'd never be ready to be a hero.

"Mom said not to bother him with *questions,*" Odd said, her voice muffled through her hands. "This isn't a question; this is an emergency."

Even waffled for another minute, and then, with a sigh, she slid off the bed and plopped onto the floor. "Fine. You're right." Of course they had to tell him, and of course she had to swallow her pride and ask him to change her back. She couldn't take the exam like this. The Academy would never pass a girl who was stuck as a skunk.

"Wait! You can't track that smell through the house!" Odd rushed across the room, yanked the sheets off Even's bed, and ran past Even to the bathroom. Even heard the faucet turn on and followed her sister, who was shoving all the sheets in the tub. "You get in too," Odd ordered.

Even opened her mouth to argue. Odd had just said this was an emergency!

But Odd's eyes were watering, and she did not look open to negotiation. Even knew that mood — if she wanted Odd's help, she'd have to cooperate. And Even did want her sister's help. *I'm not telling Dad by myself,* Even thought. Someone had to help her explain it wasn't her fault. Or at least not entirely her fault. She'd tried to change herself back.

Even hopped into the bathtub and landed on top of her sheets.

Odd checked her phone. "Dish soap and baking soda for skunk odor. Okay, we have those. Do *not* leave the tub." She darted out and returned in less than a minute. Kneeling beside the tub, she dumped baking soda into the water and squirted Palmolive on top of Even's fur. "You couldn't have changed into a squirrel or a cat or anything else?"

"Sorry." Squatting, Even submerged herself up to her neck as the tub filled with water. She wished they could fix this without involving Dad. "Can *you* change me back? It's an odd day."

"What? No!" Odd nearly dropped the dish soap. "You know

me. I'd be just as likely to change you into a toaster. Or a labradoodle."

"You know you can't change me into a toaster. Living things can only become other living things. Basic transformation theory. And a labradoodle would be better than a skunk. Come on, can't you try?" The key to transformation was familiarity —you had to be able to picture your goal as clearly as possible. *Surely Odd can picture what I look like well enough,* Even thought. It wasn't as if she didn't have the ability. After all, they shared the same magic. It bound them together even more firmly than sharing toothpaste.

"There's a really good reason Mom always changes you back after I skunk you," Odd said. "I can do a random skunk, but getting a specific person with all the right details? What if I mess up?"

"Just try. Please!"

"Fine. But no promises. If you end up a labradoodle, you can't blame me." Odd concentrated. Her forehead crinkled as she stared at Even. Finally, she exhaled and said, "It didn't work."

"Did you picture me?"

"Of course I pictured you! And before you ask, *not* as a skunk."

Even climbed over the wet sheets to the water spilling out of the faucet and rinsed the dish soap out of her fur. She scrambled up to the side of the tub. Ugh, the wet fur felt awful. Heavy with water, it pulled at her skin. "Can you help me with a towel?"

Odd grabbed a towel and laid it next to the tub.

Even jumped onto it and tried rolling around to dry herself. "Odd? More help?"

"This is both absurd and scary, and it's entirely your fault," Odd said as she rubbed Even's fur with the towel. When she finished, she sat back.

Looking down at her still-damp fur, Even shivered. "Hair dryer?"

"Absurd *and* scary," Odd repeated. But she got the hair dryer, plugged it in, and blew hot air at Even's fur.

Leaning toward the dryer, Even felt the warmth seep through her fur and into her skin, and she sighed in relief. *From here on, I'm going to feel bad for every single skunk, squirrel, and rabbit out in a rainstorm.* Wet fur was decidedly more unpleasant than wet skin.

As Even's fur dried, it fluffed out around her. She hopped onto the toilet seat and then onto the counter to look in the mirror. With all her fur poofed out, she could have been mistaken for the squishiest stuffed animal ever. "Wow, I look ridiculous." She twisted, examining herself from all angles. Every bit of her was fluffy.

Odd switched off the dryer. "You look adorable. But you really, really can't stay this way, even if I want to cuddle you." She sounded on the verge of laughing. Or crying.

Even knew Odd was right. She had to find a way to fix this.

It's my responsibility. I'm the older sister. I'm the one who wants to be a hero and help people. And I'm the one who made this mess. "I didn't know I'd get stuck as a skunk. This never happened before! Can you try again? Please?"

Concentrating on her, Odd tried again.

Even waited to feel a tingling in her skin. She imagined her bones stretching and her muscles stretching and her face changing . . . but she felt absolutely nothing.

What if . . .

No, that can't be right.

But what if . . .

"Make me fly," Even suggested.

"How will that help? I don't think a flying skunk is the best idea—"

"Just . . . I want to test a theory," Even said. "Please, Odd. I know this is weird, and you don't know what to do, but please make me fly. Or the soap. Make something fly. It's easy magic. You've been doing it for years."

It was so easy that sometimes Odd made things fly when she didn't want to. Like the puppy in the shelter. And a few months ago, Odd had come home from school in tears because she had accidentally levitated a pint of chocolate milk in the cafeteria—crashing it directly into the assistant principal. Like at the shelter, everyone had thought she'd thrown it. It had taken Mom and Dad both going into school, insisting it had been an accident and that she'd really been trying to toss it into the trash can, to get Odd out of detention. She'd had to practice extra to prove she was ready to go back to school. And now she'd have to practice more before Mom and Dad allowed her to go back to the shelter on odd days.

Scowling at the soap, Odd wrinkled her forehead. A few seconds later, she exhaled. "It's not working. That's—"

"Weird, I know."

"Great!" Odd switched to staring at a bottle of shampoo, then the roll of toilet paper, then a box of tissues. "This means I can go to the shelter today! I can help with the kittens! This is—"

Even laid a paw on Odd's leg. "Don't say 'great' again."

"Oh. Sorry. I forgot."

"You forgot I'm a skunk. Just now. While I'm standing here on four paws." Shaking the last of the moisture out of her tail, Even led the way to the bathroom door. "We need to tell Dad. If my magic *and* your magic are both having issues . . ."

After shutting off the water in the tub, Odd left the sheets soaking and followed her. "Well, my magic *is* your magic. Makes sense that if yours is on the fritz, mine would be too."

"But why? What's wrong with us?"

Slowing, Even peeked into their parents' bedroom. She wished Mom were home. Mom knew much more about how their magic worked than Dad did. He'd always been more interested in magical artifacts, like cursed amulets, magic mirrors, and enchanted furniture. He was less likely to know what to do.

"Maybe Dad can call Mom," Even said.

"He has her itinerary," Odd agreed. "He'll know how to direct the mirror."

Letting themselves into the shop through the back door, they heard voices. Dad wasn't alone. Stopping among the shelves in the supply closet, they listened. Even recognized two of the non-Dad voices: Frank the researcher and the elven high priestess.

Oh no! Not her again!

She couldn't talk to Dad now. Not in front of *her!* Even didn't know if she was terrified, mortified, or some horrible mix of the two. She had to resist the urge to burrow into the floor with her front claws and hide from everyone.

"You were able to un-curse my amulet," the elf said. Her voice was haughty, as if she were used to commanding a legion of servants and had never heard "no," which Even thought was possibly accurate. "I don't see why you cannot assist with this problem."

"It's not that I don't want to help—" Dad said.

A new voice bleated, "You have to help!"

"The child is correct," the elf said. "I have waited for the problem to solve itself naturally, but I am through with patience. You must assist us."

Creeping forward, Even peeked out of the closet. She saw Dad pressed against the cash register with a stiff, panicked smile on his face. Frank the centaur was pacing back and forth—he could only go two steps before he had to turn around. The elf priestess had her robes wrapped tightly around her, and she was scowling so hard that she almost looked to be vibrating. Closer to the supply closet—close enough that Even could see his shimmering white pelt, golden spiral horn, and the pink satchel that dangled around his neck—was a unicorn.

Whoa, a unicorn! In their shop! Amazing! She'd never seen one in person before . . . And then she remembered she wasn't "in person." Why did all the cool visitors have to come when she was in the middle of a crisis?

"Been doing this for six months," Frank was saying. "Never had trouble sending my reports back across the border, 'specially not for this long. But you've been here for years. Ever seen anything like this?"

"I haven't, and that's why—" Dad said.

"*You* run the border shop," the elf said. "*You* are the expert. *You* must fix the gateway."

"It's not my area of expertise."

Poor Dad, Even thought. He sounded like he wanted to bolt. She knew the feeling. She certainly never wanted to talk to the elf again. But wait—what did she mean by "fix the gateway"?

"Who, then?" the elf demanded. "You advertise that you

service the needs of all travelers. This is my need! My daughter's first Moonlight Dance is tomorrow night, an important rite of passage, and she needs her mother to be present. I must return home, present her with her gift, and be with her for this life moment! I cannot be stuck here in this magicless world, without access to my powers."

"And I have to go home too!" the unicorn cried.

Behind her, Odd whispered, "What's going on?"

"I don't know," Even whispered back. "The elf priestess said Dad has to fix the gateway. Guess it's not acting right? The unicorn and the elf are both having trouble going home." And Frank wasn't able to send his report through. He usually attached them to enchanted paper birds. She'd seen them flying toward the gateway—they looked like origami seagulls.

"What do you mean? What's wrong with the gateway?"

Even didn't know. She'd never heard of the gateway not allowing someone through. You just had to know where one was hidden, and you could cross. No spells needed. No potions used. No special ritual. You just walked through the arch. Mom said it tickled a little. Some people threw up.

"If there's something wrong with the gateway," Odd asked, "how does Mom get home?"

That was a horrifying question. If the elf and unicorn were having difficulty crossing from the mundane world to the magical world, could people in the magical world cross back to the mundane world? What if the gateway was malfunctioning in both directions?

"I don't know," Even whispered.

In the shop, the customers were getting more and more worked up. "Can't stay here if my disguise spell won't work," Frank was saying. "And Ms. Pointy Ears here isn't much less conspicuous without her magical glamour."

The elf sniffed. "Excuse me? 'Pointy Ears'? How would you like it if I identified you by a physical attribute, Horse Boy?"

"Eh, it's accurate. If the horseshoe fits, wear it, Pointy Ears."

"At least we're not the only ones having trouble with magic," Even said to Odd. Frank's spells weren't working, and the elf wasn't able to use her powers. In a way it was a relief to hear that others were having issues too. That meant it wasn't something wrong with her and Odd's shared magic, or at least it wasn't *just* that. Lots of magic was on the fritz.

"Definitely not just us," Odd said. "If magic isn't working *and* the gateway isn't working . . ."

"Can't be a coincidence."

They were still whispering, though it wasn't necessary given how loudly the elf was proclaiming her demands. She'd clearly decided that Dad knew how to help and he was just being stubborn about it. She was alternating between promising him riches and threatening him with curses.

"In order to work magic, you have to be born with the ability to use it," Even said, thinking out loud, "but the magic itself —the actual *oomph*—comes from the magic world, specifically through the border . . ."

"Everyone knows that," Odd said. "Just because I don't study as much as you do doesn't mean . . . Oh." Her eyes widened as she realized the implications of Even's words. "You think it's all connected. You think"—she swallowed hard—"magic isn't working *because* the gateway is broken. You think the border is, essentially, closed."

The unicorn shoved his head into the closet. "What? It can't be!"

Startled, Even felt her tail fly up, and out came another puff of stench.

5

AS SOON AS the scent of skunk spread into the shop, Dad shooed everyone out. He and the customers fled outside, behind several strategically placed large bushes, while Even and Odd retreated into the laundry room.

"What do we do?" Odd said.

"I don't know —"

Squeezing into the laundry room with them, the unicorn craned his neck to study the laundry detergent as if it were the most fascinating thing he'd ever seen. He barely fit between the dryer and the linen closet.

Whoa, now the real, live unicorn was in their house! Even had dreamed of meeting a unicorn ever since she'd first learned about them. She just wished he'd come any other day. "Not to be rude, but who are you?" she asked.

"You can call me Jeremy."

"Jeremy?" Even repeated. "Your name is Jeremy?" That

was . . . "Really?" She'd been told that unicorns had names like Sparkle or Glitterhoof or Sunbeam the Everlasting. They were supposed to be the pinnacle of purity and nobility.

"Well, it's not my real name. I'm here in secret." He turned his head sideways into the shadows, as if trying to appear mysterious. Unfortunately, the shadows were made by Dad's boxers, drying on the line above the washing machine, so he failed to look impressive. He looked, well, silly. And squished.

"Okay, great to meet you, Jeremy," Even said. Any other time, she'd have had a thousand questions, such as why a magical being whose species was known to be unable to lie was trying to go anywhere in secret, but right now she only wanted to talk with Odd. "Really, really sorry, but could you please wait here until Dad reopens the shop? We have a family emergency."

She backed out of the laundry room tail first, and Odd followed her into the kitchen. Pancake batter still dotted the counter and floor.

Jeremy followed too, holding his breath as he squeezed through. "I have an emergency too!" he said. "A serious emergency."

He didn't seem to be bleeding or have any broken bones. She thought her problems trumped his right now. "Oh?" Even asked. "No offense, but are you stuck in a shape that's not your own, unable to control what comes out of your rear end?"

He pawed the floor with his hoof. "Um, no. But I can poop cupcakes."

Well, *that* was enough to distract her. Even felt her furry jaw drop open. She wanted to ask how that was possible. Especially if they had icing. "You suddenly began pooping cupcakes? When did this start? Was it yesterday? Because that's when I—"

"Oh no, I've always done it. When I was a foal, they were chocolate cupcakes, but now that I'm older, they're lemon-strawberry, with buttercream icing."

Even and Odd both gawked at him.

"Wait," Even said. "If you've always done it, why is it an emergency?"

"It's not," Jeremy said. "But it smells delicious."

"That's . . ." Even couldn't think of what word she wanted to use. *Disgusting*? *Amazing*? "Irrelevant." There was an actual emergency going on. Did he not get that? Pooping cupcakes didn't have anything to do with a malfunctioning gateway.

"Sorry." Jeremy's head drooped. "That wasn't really appropriate, was it? It's just . . . when I'm stressed, I'm not very good at talking. And I'm very stressed. I'm not supposed to be here."

"Then why are you here?" Even asked.

"I came to this glorious world *clandestinely*." He said it as if he'd just learned the word, and he swung his head fast to the right and left for emphasis, knocking a kitchen towel off its perch with his horn. "Oops. Sorry," he said again. "I came to explore. And also to purchase soda and a new pack of cards for Farmcats, my favorite game."

"You play Farmcats?" Odd said at the same time as Even said, "You bought soda?"

"I love soda, and love Farmcats," Jeremy said. "Earlier, I bought six cans of Sprite and a brand-new Farmcats deck from the border store. Got them in my pack." Shaking his mane, he showed off his pink sparkly satchel. It was specially shaped to fit over his horned head and drape across his neck—in essence, a unicorn backpack.

"But why soda?" Even wondered if he knew that soda was the key to negating magic in magical artifacts. It wasn't a secret, but her parents didn't advertise the truth, either. Dad said it drew more business to the shop if everyone thought un-cursings were complex. Could the unicorn have a cursed amulet, necklace, sword, stone . . . or backpack?

"I like the bubbles."

"And the cards?" Odd pressed. "How do you play a card game with hooves? And how have you even heard of it? I thought it was a mundane-world game."

"A cousin of mine who travels bought me my first pack of cards at a border store last year. I can flip the cards with my teeth." He showed them his horselike teeth. "And I move them with my hoof. Why do you care what I bought? You aren't my parents. It's not your business."

"Technically, it *is* our business," Odd said. "Our family owns the border store."

"Ah, then if it's your store, you can help me!" Jeremy said. "Border stores are supposed to help any magical creature visiting the mundane world. Everyone knows that. It's in your advertisements."

Even hadn't seen any of their ads for herself, but she was sure he was right. Mom's business trips were designed to spread exactly that message as widely as she could. *I guess it makes sense that he's here, even if it doesn't make sense that he likes soda and poops cupcakes.* "Do you actually have an emergency?"

"Yes! Weren't you paying attention? I have to get home! My parents don't know I'm here, and they're going to be so mad at me!"

Even tilted her head back to stare at him. He was much larger than her skunk self, but he still didn't seem full-grown. He fit in the laundry room, though it was a tight squeeze. *He can't be . . .* But yes, he was. Unicorn or not, he was just a kid afraid of getting in trouble with his parents. "You really play Farmcats?"

"It's an excellent game."

"It is," Odd agreed. She played it with her friends from school all the time. Even had never seen the appeal. And she certainly couldn't imagine why a unicorn who lived in a world with magic all around him would be interested in a card game about cats, roosters, and malfunctioning farm equipment—so interested that he'd defy his parents and sneak across the border into another world.

Even shook her head. "This is all so very wrong. Out of curiosity, how old are you?"

"In unicorn years or human years?"

"Unicorn, I guess."

"Nine," he said.

"And human years?"

"Well, it doesn't directly translate . . ."

Even asked bluntly, "Are you a kid?"

"I'm old enough! My parents trust me on errands to New City all the time!"

He was just a kid. He sounded far too defensive about the question to be anything but. *And he's stuck on the wrong side of the border,* she thought. *Scared, and trying not to be.*

She wasn't at all surprised that Odd patted his neck and said in the same tone she used for nervous puppies at the shelter, "Don't worry. We'll take care of you."

"I don't need taking care of." He drew himself up taller, as if that would make him appear older. Instead it made him look like he was going to tip over. "I just . . . don't know what to do."

The last bit was said in such a small voice that Even felt sorry for him.

"How about we ask Dad if we can use the magic mirror, and you can call the Academy of Magic?" Even suggested. "Tell them you're having trouble getting home, and ask them what to do." The Academy was designed to solve all magical problems. Surely, they'd be able to help.

"What? No! Terrible idea!" Jeremy said. "I can't talk to them! They're the Academy! They're important! I'll end up putting my hoof in my mouth and look like a silly kid who can't be trusted to do anything! And anyway, they'd tell my parents immediately. Besides, I know I'd say it all wrong. I told you: I'm not good at talking to people. Especially grownups."

"You were just talking to our dad," Odd said.

"I was *panicking* at your dad," Jeremy said. "There's a difference. Isn't there something else we could do to get me back across the border? *Clandestinely?*"

Even could understand not wanting to get in trouble. She glanced at her furry paws and thought about her decision to hide her transformation problem from Dad.

"Well, if the border is closed," Even said, thinking out loud, "that would explain all of this: why I'm still a skunk, why our magic isn't working, and why Jeremy can't get home. So I guess the first thing is to find out if that's what's going on. Is there a problem with the gateway, or is there a problem with us?"

Odd nodded. "Yeah, someone needs to check out the gateway."

"Great! Much better idea! I can do that. Is this the way out?" Jeremy trotted to the front door.

"Wait, you can't!" Odd yelped. "Someone will see you!"

"Can't wait! The longer I wait, the more likely my parents will find out. Or someone 'helpful' will tell them." He bit the doorknob, twisted it to open, and pushed himself through. His hindquarters got stuck. Wiggling, he freed himself and popped out onto the front steps.

Even and Odd exchanged glances and then hurried out. "You can't just wander around outside," Odd said behind him. "There are people who don't know about the magical world. A lot of people. And we're supposed to keep it that way."

"It's better if you stay inside," Even called. "Let a grownup handle it."

Crossing the lawn, he trampled the flower beds. "My grown-ups aren't here! And I have to get back to them as soon as I can!"

Even and Odd chased after him.

From the driveway, Dad called, "Unicorn, where are you going? Odd, what's — Even, is that you? Are you still a skunk?"

Even chose not to answer that last question, since it was both obvious and obviously embarrassing. "He's going to check the gateway!"

"Excellent idea!" Dad said. "Someone should do that!" He

started toward them, but he was stopped by the elf priestess. Stepping in front of him, she put his hand on his chest.

"You will assist *me*," the elf said, "before you go hurrying off without a plan. Let the pony run your errand while you attend to my needs."

Joining Frank, several other centaurs clustered around Dad. They clamored for his attention. "Our magic isn't functioning—" "We tried to send a message—" "Our colleague was supposed to come through—"

"One at a time," Dad pleaded with them.

Even hesitated for a second. She'd expected Dad to jump in and take control of the situation with Jeremy and the gateway, but he couldn't. Not with the elf and the centaurs demanding his help. *They're not interested in me, though,* she thought. *I could do it.* "Odd and I can go, Dad!" She glanced at Odd to make sure she didn't mind being volunteered. She didn't seem to. "We can get the unicorn there and report back on what we find!"

"Yes, please. Thank you, Even! Thank you, Odd!" He ran his hands through his rainbow hair. "Consider it your first quest! Make sure he isn't seen. And be careful!"

Even felt her fur fluff proudly around her. Of course she knew it wasn't a *real* quest—it was just a trip to the bagel store —but she still liked the sound of it. And she liked that Dad was trusting them to help.

"Cool. First quest," Odd said, decidedly unexcited. "Yay. So what do we do, O Great Skunky Hero? How do we make sure no one sees him?"

The unicorn hadn't slowed. He was already clopping down the middle of the street.

Even considered it briefly. "Get your bike. We can stay off the roads if we stick to the bike path. If anyone comes, we hide Jeremy behind a tree." It wasn't the perfect plan, but given that the unicorn was already halfway across the cul-de-sac, it had to do.

Odd hurried to retrieve her bike from beside the house. When she came back, she lifted Even into the basket. "You can't be seen either," she said. "Duck down if anyone comes." Odd began pedaling to catch up with Jeremy. "If the animal shelter finds out I'm transporting a wild animal—that's you right now, sorry—in a bike basket, they're not going to trust me around their rescues. I can't even imagine what they'd say about the unicorn. Irresponsible horse care, at best. They'll think I glued a horn on his head. It's not like I can tell them I now have magical-animal sidekicks."

"We won't let anyone from this world see us," Even promised. "And I am *not* your sidekick—though, yes, I get that I look like one." She wished there were a less embarrassing way to travel than hidden in a bike basket. If she had her magic, she could have flown there. Or transformed into a bird. Or changed back into a human and ridden her own bike. She squeezed herself into the basket, curling up with her tail around her.

Peering out through the weave of the basket, Even checked the street. Their house was on a heavily wooded cul-de-sac with two other houses, both owned by emigrants from Firoth, so it was relatively safe to be out in the open here. Once on the path, though, they'd have to keep an eye out for joggers or anyone walking their dog, baby, or whatever.

"Wait for us!" Odd called to the unicorn.

Miraculously, he waited.

The closest house belonged to a centaur, Mr. Nessus, who was a member of Frank's research group. Outside his house, he used an illusion spell to make his horse half look like really muscular human legs, but if he couldn't maintain the glamour, he'd be stuck inside. Not a pleasant fate for someone who was half horse.

Strangely, the second house was dark. The fairies who lived there *never* shut off the lights—bright bulbs hid their magic-fueled glow. But she didn't see any sign of either artificial or fairy light, even though she knew the fairies had to be there —they never left. They were, alarmingly, lightless.

She felt a shiver run through her fur. No one's magic was working.

Catching up with Jeremy, Odd called, "This way!" She led him toward the bike path.

In the basket, Even kept worrying. She'd never heard of this happening before. How serious was this? How concerned should she be? How long was it going to last? How long was she going to be stuck as a skunk? How was Mom going to get home?

Peering out again, Even glimpsed a flash of pink up ahead. She poked her nose over the lip of the basket to see better: it was a runner in pink leggings. "Jogger coming," she whisper-shouted. "Jeremy, hide!"

Slowing, Odd shooed Jeremy into the bushes. He crashed into the shrubbery with less grace than a rhinoceros as the jogger came into view: a young woman with a ponytail and ear-buds. She nodded, barely glancing at them, as she ran by.

They waited a few seconds.

"You can come out," Odd called softly to Jeremy.

He trotted out of the bushes and onto the path. Shaking his head, he tossed off stray leaves and branches that had stuck to his mane. An oak leaf was impaled on his horn. "That was close! Maybe we should go back."

"We already told Dad we'd check the gateway," Even said.

Odd plucked the leaf off his horn. "You just need to hide whenever we see someone."

"This is more stressful than I thought it would be."

"It was your idea," Odd told him.

"Maybe it was a bad one. You were right—someone *could* see me. Someone who doesn't know about Firoth. Or unicorns. Someone who—"

"Just stick with us," Even said. "It's not far."

They continued on, and Jeremy had to plunge into the bushes three more times: for a man jogging with a stroller of twin babies, for a high schooler on a skateboard, and for three elderly women power walking down the bike path. Even squished herself into the basket as deeply as she could each time, while the unicorn concealed himself in the thick weeds and underbrush.

Miraculously, they made it to the end of the bike path without incident.

Odd quit pedaling. Pressing her eyes close to the gaps in the basket weave, Even looked out at the intersection. Cars passed by steadily. Across the street, beyond the traffic light, was a strip mall with a CVS, a bank, and Fratelli's Express Bagel. Behind the bagel store, hidden from view, was the gateway.

"How are we going to cross?" Odd asked. Even could hear the nervousness in Odd's voice and knew her sister was imagining a hundred terrible scenarios.

Even wanted to tell her not to worry, it would all be okay, but she thought she might lack credibility, given that she was a skunk.

"Ooh, what is that?" Jeremy poked his head past Odd's.

She shooed him back. "A traffic light."

"It looks like a 2019 Ford Mustang GT. Cherry red with a V8 engine. *Vroom-vroom!*"

"Okay, sure, but—"

Even interrupted. "Jeremy has to stay here and keep himself hidden."

"What? But you just said to stick with you! You can't leave me here by myself! I'm supposed to go with you to the gateway —and home!"

"Sorry, buddy," Odd said. "She's right. You'll be seen."

He snorted at her. "Not if I use my invisibility cloak."

Rising up onto her hind legs to glare at him better, Even considered spraying him for being this unbelievably irritating when, as a unicorn, he was supposed to be wise and magical and delightful. "You had an invisibility cloak *this whole time?*"

"Um, yes?" he said, as if he wasn't sure why she sounded upset. "In my pack. I used it to cushion the soda."

Even wasn't sure whether to be relieved or annoyed. She decided on both.

6

'EVEN PEERED ACROSS the street at the bagel store, while Jeremy used his teeth to yank his cloak out of his satchel. So far no one had come in or out of the store, which was unusual. It should have had a line out the door, until they ran out of bagels around noon. It was the most popular bagel spot in Stony Haven. There were two others, but only Fratelli's had the French toast bagels with powdered sugar.

It was also the only one owned by a wizard, which Even did not think was a coincidence. French toast bagels tasted magically delicious.

A car pulled into the parking lot, and Even watched a woman get out, try the door, fail to open it, and then return to her car and drive away. "I think Fratelli's is closed," Even said.

"Do you think it's because of the gateway?" Odd asked.

"He uses magic to bake his bagels. So, yeah, if he doesn't have anything to sell, it makes sense he'd close the store." *He must be really upset,* she thought. It was clear how much he loved his store. He always wore a huge smile while he chatted with the customers and baked his magically delicious bagels. Whenever Even had gone in with Mom, he'd greeted them with the jolliest smile. Like a carb-and-cream-cheese-bearing Santa Claus.

She glanced back to see if Jeremy was ready. He poked his head under the cloak, tossed it over his body, and vanished beneath it. "Ta-da!" he said. "How do I look? Or *not* look?"

"Perfect," Even said.

"Not quite." Odd pointed down.

Peeking over the edge of the basket, Even looked where her sister was pointing: four clearly visible hooves. The invisibility cloak only covered the unicorn's body. It didn't reach all the way down to his hooves. "It doesn't fit you."

Jeremy's voice floated from what looked like empty air. "Well, it's not technically mine, but I didn't steal it!"

"I know you can't lie," Odd said. "Otherwise, that sounded super suspicious."

"Stealing implies you have no intention of giving it back," Jeremy said. "I borrowed without permission." He sounded very pleased with himself for thinking of this distinction.

"Stick close to the bike," Even said. "People will think it just has strange wheels. No one's going to see his hooves and think, 'Oh, that must be a mostly invisible unicorn.'" Or at least she hoped that was true. In her experience, people were very eager to explain away the unexplainable. But she knew Odd worried about people's reactions a lot.

"They'll think I'm doing something strange again." Odd sighed. "You'd think no magic would mean I'd get to have a normal day. But of course not." She got back on the bike.

"At least you aren't a skunk."

"One thing I'm grateful for. I need another four."

"You're helping a young unicorn," Even said.

Odd perked up. "You're right. That's nearly as good as helping kittens."

Even hid herself in the basket again. Peering through the weave, she watched as they emerged from the bike path and waited for the traffic light. When it changed, Odd pedaled across, while Jeremy kept pace beside them. They passed the CVS and the bank and then the bagel store.

Inside, Fratelli's was dark, and only the shadows of the cream cheese case and the shelves were visible. Even didn't see any movement, and the bagel shelves appeared to be empty, which was tragic.

She wondered where Mr. Fratelli was. He had a daughter who went to school in the magic world. With the gateway not working, he wouldn't be able to contact her. He must have been worried.

She tried to convince herself she wasn't worried about Mom.

As they rounded the corner, Even saw Mom's car parked in the employee lot, and she wondered if Mom had any idea there was something wrong on this side of the border. If they were lucky, everything would be all back to normal, including Even's non-skunky self, before Mom even thought about coming home.

Odd braked and dismounted. She leaned the bike against a dumpster. "We made it."

"Can I take off the cloak?" Jeremy asked. "It's itchy."

"No one can see us back here," Even reassured him. "That's why the gateway is here. Not visible from either the street or the parking lot." She waved at the brick wall—the *empty* brick wall, where the gateway was supposed to be.

Guess that explains why no one can get through, she thought.

She shivered, and the shiver ruffled all her fur. What had happened to the gateway? She'd never heard of it just disappearing.

Beside them, Jeremy shook off his invisibility cloak and used his teeth and nose to stuff it into his satchel. Even hopped out of the basket onto the ground. Sniffing the air as if she could sniff out the missing gateway, she inhaled the sour stench of garbage. Shaking her head, she sneezed, trying to get the stench—worse than anything she'd ever smelled—out of her sensitive skunk nostrils.

Much taller than they were, Jeremy stuck his head into the

dumpster. "Whoa, this is cool. You know, in the magic world, we don't have trash because of the pixies. They eat it. Pixies eat everything. They're worse than rats. At least rats don't have wings. Well, most of them."

"You have rats with wings?" Even said, momentarily distracted from staring at the empty space where the gateway was supposed to be. How many other creatures were there in the magic world that she'd never heard of? She'd peppered her parents with questions over the years, but there was still so much she didn't know.

"Where's the gateway?" Odd asked.

That pulled Even's attention back to where it was supposed to be.

"It's usually—" Even was going to say *right here* and nod pointedly at the blank brick wall, but then, suddenly, in the time between Odd's question and her answer, it *was* there: a shimmering between the bricks, as if they were held together by glitter glue instead of mortar. "Huh, it looks fine."

There were multiple gateways throughout the world, existing at fixed points, such as behind Fratelli's Express Bagels. On the other side, in Firoth, they were part of the border itself, embedded in an otherwise impenetrable wall of mist. In the mundane world, you could always recognize a gateway by the way it sparkled. And here it was, sparkling.

"What does this mean?" Jeremy asked. "Is it working again? Is everything okay? Can I go home?"

Could it be that simple? Had the gateway fixed itself?

"Odd, try to do something magical," Even said.

Squinching her face in concentration, Odd focused on the dumpster. Even held her breath as a half-eaten bagel rose out of the trash. It wobbled in the air, but it was undoubtedly floating. Exhaling, she cheered.

The bagel crashed back into the dumpster as Odd's concentration broke.

"Sorry," Odd said. "I lost it."

"Not the point." Even shook her tail in excitement. "You did magic!" Whatever was wrong seemed to have fixed itself. This was excellent news! "Transform me back into myself."

Odd hesitated. "I don't think that's a good idea."

Even hopped from paw to paw. "Just try. I know you can do it! Just picture me as me — not, you know, as a skunk or a snake or whatever." If she could return home as herself, then they could go on with everything as usual. Dad would be so happy. She could be the one to tell him, Frank, and the elven high priestess that the gateway was fixed. Or she and Odd could tell them together. Sisters united, triumphant!

Taking a deep breath, Odd focused on her.

Even felt her skin tingle. Her fur began to vibrate. *Yes! She's doing it!*

Her fur smoothed, and Even twisted, trying to see as much of herself as she could. Her own skin should be appearing . . . She felt herself stretch and thin, lengthening as if she were play dough pushed through a tube. Scales burst out over her body, and her legs were sucked up into her belly. She felt as if her arms were tied too tight to her sides and her legs were glued together. Lying on the ground, she looked up at Odd. Her tongue slid back and forth between two snake fangs. She shouldn't have said the word "snake." "Maybe try again?" she suggested. "Pleassssssse?"

Odd's hands flew to her mouth in horror. "I'm so sorry! I can fix this. Maybe." Concentrating again, she began to tremble, as if she were squeezing every muscle in her body.

Even felt the familiar tickling. Limbs burst out of her body, and the scales merged into smooth skin. She felt herself rising up onto four legs, higher and higher. A shimmering white hide covered her body. Her forehead ached as a horn burst out from the center of it.

Now Jeremy's exact height, she stared into his eyes.

"Wow," he said.

Reflected in his eyes was a matching unicorn.

"You look awesome."

Twisting her head, Even saw her unicorn body, gleaming white. She felt a heaviness in the center of her forehead. Her horn? "I can't stay like this. There's only one invisibility cloak."

She couldn't cross the street looking like a unicorn, as cool as that was, and she didn't relish the idea of spending the night hiding behind the bagel store. "One more try, Odd?"

Odd was concentrating hard, with her hands clenched by her sides and her face squinched up. "I don't think I can do it! I'm so sorry!"

"Just one more try. Please?"

Again, Odd concentrated. Even felt the tingle yet again as she shrank rapidly back down toward the pavement. Her pelt grew, lengthening to long black-and-white fur. Her hooves reshaped into paws, and her horselike tail fluffed out into a skunk tail.

Odd slumped against the dumpster. "I'm really sorry, Even."

She should have known better than to ask. Odd never practiced, and this was the result. Shuddering, Even remembered how it had felt to be an armless and legless snake. *If only it was an even day!* she thought. "Actually, this might be your best skunk yet — this is definitely your magical specialty," Even said, trying to cheer her up.

Odd let out a shaky laugh. "Yeah. As if that's a skill I'll ever need."

"I think you made my tail even more magnificent than ever. And things could be a lot worse." Shimmering, the gateway still looked like it was supposed to. And at least Odd's magic was as functional as it ever was. Everything was fixed! Probably.

Unless it wasn't. "How do we know it's really fixed? I mean, it *looks* okay, but what if it's not?"

Jeremy pranced anxiously. "What if it just *looks* like it's working and you step through and hit the brick wall? Or what if it sends you to the wrong place, like the top of a mountain or bottom of an ocean? Or what if it turns you into an avocado?"

"It can't turn you into an avocado," Even said. "It's a door."

"Well, it could still be broken."

That much was true.

All three of them stared at the gateway, hoping it would do something to prove everything really was back to normal. She didn't want to rush home with the good news and then find out that it still wouldn't let anyone pass. She could just imagine what the elf high priestess would say about her then. It would be worse than "foolish" and "frivolous." But if Even could find out whether the gateway was operational or not, that could be useful.

There was, of course, one way to prove everything was back to normal.

"We could test it," Even said.

Odd reacted exactly as Even expected her to. "What? No! Absolutely not!"

"I don't want to go back to Dad and the customers, say it's fixed, and then find out we're wrong." A hero would see the task all the way through. Not that she was a hero yet, but still . . . If she wanted to be one someday, she should practice acting like one.

"Admit it," Odd said, "you just want to see the magic world."

That wasn't it! Okay, it was a little bit that. But her curiosity was far from the only reason. "I don't just want to see the magic world!" Even felt her tail fluffing up, and she took a deep breath. *No spraying,* she ordered herself. The air already stank enough from the dumpster. "Look, if we go home and say, 'It's working!' and we're right, then we've done something useful. But if we go home and say, 'I don't know, maybe it's fixed; we went all the way there but didn't test it,' then who does that help?"

"It doesn't have to be you," Odd said. "Let Jeremy go through. He can report back."

Even opened her mouth to object, but she couldn't think of an argument. Asking him to test the gateway was the logical choice. Sure, she wanted to see the magic world, but she wanted to do the right thing even more. "Jeremy—"

"Oh no. If I make it home, I definitely can't come back," Jeremy said. He gave a little shudder, shaking his mane. "I'm not supposed to be here in the first place. Besides, what if it doesn't work? Or what if it does work and my parents are waiting for me on the other side? What if they confiscate my Farmcats cards? What if—"

"All we want is for you to check—" Odd began.

Cutting her off, Even said, "It's okay. He doesn't have to do it. I'll cross, see if it works, and be back before either of you even miss me." She trotted toward the shimmering brick wall. She'd just take a peek at the other world. One peek. And then she'd return.

"You could run into trouble," Odd said. "It's an odd day. You don't have magic. I'll do it."

She had a point, but . . . "I'm the one training to be a hero." And it was Even's idea. That made it feel like it was her responsibility. "I'll do it."

"We do it together," Odd said.

Even liked the sound of that. "Together."

Odd picked up Even and held her in her arms. "Coming, Jeremy? You said you wanted to go home." She took a step toward the gateway. Then another. Even began quivering with a mix of nervousness and excitement.

What if it didn't work?

It has to work! she thought. After all, Odd had magic again. Even told herself there wasn't anything to worry about. This was just a test to be sure. *We'll cross the border, confirm that everything is okay, and come back.* Once they were home, Dad would be able to de-skunkify her. Everything would be back to normal soon.

Odd halted. "Maybe this is a bad idea. I don't think I—"

"Together!" Jeremy cried. He bumped into her back with his shoulder, and they all fell toward the shimmering brick wall. And through it.

7

EVEN FELT A tickle all over her skin, beneath her fur, and then the tickle sharpened as if she were being poked by a thousand tiny thorns. She couldn't hear anything, smell anything, taste anything . . . For one terrible minute, she thought, *This is it: I'm dead.*

She tumbled onto the grass head over tail and landed on her back looking up at an alien sky.

"Whoa," she said.

It was still blue, but it wasn't the same kind of blue she was used to—it was closer to a sea blue, with streaks of green and black within the clouds. The air tasted different too, like cinnamon and burned sugar.

I remember this taste, she thought. How could she have forgotten it? Breathing in, she remembered moments: running to her dad and having him magically fly her around the room like a kite, and building a sandcastle on a windy day — the sand kept scattering until Mom transformed her castle into crystal. The sandy wind had smelled like this. She wished she could remember more.

She rolled onto her paws and stood, shaking out her fur. "Odd?" Even called.

"Here!" Odd sat up a few feet away. Her usually stick-straight hair was frizzed in all directions, as if full of static electricity. She patted it down, but it sprang back up. "Sorry I dropped you. That was so weird. I couldn't feel anything."

"Me either." She felt normal now, though, or at least as normal as she could, given that she was a skunk. She tested her legs and swished her tail. "Jeremy? Are you okay?"

The unicorn was frolicking across the meadow, kicking up his hooves and tossing his mane. "Yay, yay, yay! Not doomed! Not dead!"

Even grinned. They'd done it! They'd crossed the border into Firoth, the world where magic was born. *And where I was born!* If it were an even day, she'd be able to feel it vibrating beneath her skin. As it was, it was enough to know that the magic was here and, with the gateway open, would flow back into the mundane world again too. Tomorrow she'd be able to change herself back to human. *If Dad hasn't fixed me already,* she thought. After all, she didn't have to hide her failure to transform anymore, since it wasn't her fault.

"So it's working?" Odd asked. "Everything's okay again? And Mom can come home?"

"Everything back to normal." *And soon I will be too!* Even beamed at her sister and waved her fluffy tail happily.

"Good. Really, really good. We should get back, before anything happens." Odd eyed the meadow nervously, as if it weren't the most beautiful sight that they had ever seen.

"One minute," Even begged. "Let me drink it in." The grass was a carpet of flowers: orchids, roses, and many-petaled clumps that she didn't remember ever seeing before and couldn't name. Higher than she was tall, the blades of grass tickled her belly. She rose onto her hind legs to see better. As Even watched, the petals of the nearest flowers began to spin faster and faster until the blossoms shot into the air and were carried off by the wind.

"Gah, shoo! Get off me!" Jeremy pranced in a circle, shaking off several flying flowers.

She heard giggling from within the flowers. *Flower fairies,* she thought. *Amazing!* She reached toward one and it fluttered around her paw, its petals moving as fast as a hummingbird's wings.

Then she felt a sharp prick of pain.

"Ow!" She yanked her paw back and cradled it against her furry chest. It felt like she'd gotten a flu shot right in the soft pad of her paw. A drop of blood welled up.

"Flower fairies sting," Jeremy warned her.

That would have been nice to know sooner. She glared at him, then at the flower fairies. She didn't have any memories of wasplike fairies. She licked away the drop of blood.

Odd asked Jeremy, "Are you going to get in trouble, or did we get you home soon enough? I don't think anyone saw us. Except the stinging flowers, which by the way are *not* charming." She shooed away a few with her foot.

Even agreed with her about that. She waved her skunk tail threateningly at a red-petaled fairy. It bared its tiny, needle-sharp teeth at her and then buzzed away.

"You saved me!" Jeremy neighed happily. "There's no way my parents will ever guess I was in your world. Unless I tell them. Which I don't plan to. Ever. Hey, if I make it back to your side of the border someday, how about a match of Farmcats? I think my new deck has a Mouse card."

"You're on," Odd said. She hugged him around his neck. "Really great to meet you, Jeremy. I'm glad we were able to help you get home. Ready for us to go home too, Even?"

Even knew she should say yes. Instead of speaking, she stared in every direction with eyes wide, trying to see every blade of grass and fix every detail in her memory to dissect later. She'd been so young when they'd moved that it all felt new and fresh and wondrous.

It was so, so tempting to stay longer. A few more minutes. An hour.

Reluctantly, she turned away from the meadow and faced the border. Here the gateway was an arch that floated in a wall of mist. Within the arch, a thousand liquid hues merged and shimmered. Mesmerized, she stared at the swirling colors.

"Even? We have to tell Dad the border is open. We said we would."

She's right. For her first quest to be a success, she had to complete it.

"One last second." Even inhaled deeply, wishing she could keep a bit of the burned-sugar air in her lungs, hoping she never again forgot the way it tasted, smelled, and felt.

"Seriously? You like it here? Of course you do," Odd said. "I'm happy for Jeremy's sake that the gateway worked, but this place makes my skin crawl. I can't tell what's a magic creature and what's just a plant or a cloud."

"It's every bit as incredible as I thought I remembered," Even said. She felt as if a hundred thoughts and emotions were tumbling inside her, her heart lurching like an unbalanced washing machine.

Side by side, the sisters looked at the shimmering gateway.

I'll come back, Even promised herself. This wouldn't be her last glimpse of Firoth. *Someday, I'll see it all. Someday, I'll be one of the wizards who defends it from all threats.* It just wasn't her time yet.

"Together?" Odd suggested.

"Yes, togeth—" Even began.

And the gateway vanished.

***

Both of them stared at the mist for several seconds before speaking.

"I didn't do it," Even said.

"You couldn't have done it," Odd said flatly. "It's an odd day."

They stared at the border some more.

Jeremy joined them, also staring.

"It'll come back," Odd said. "And then we'll be able to go home. We just need to wait." She said it as if it were a wish or a spell. But Even heard the note of panic in her voice. She felt the same worry, like a hand squeezing her stomach and lungs.

"Absolutely no need to be concerned," Even said, both to herself and to Odd. "This must have been what happened before. The gateway went offline temporarily, but it came back. Like you said, all we have to do is wait." She sat down and curled her tail around herself.

If it came back before, it could come back again. Right?

The three of them stared at the wall of mist. Even told herself there was nothing to panic about. It was like a power outage. You couldn't watch TV, but you could convince your parents that you'd better eat all the ice cream before it melted. Eventually, the power always returned. Eventually, the border would reopen.

Even took a deep breath and then another. *Just wait,* she told herself. The gateway would fix itself again, they'd go home, and no one would ever know how close they'd come to stranding themselves on the wrong side of the gateway. She'd take her exam on Friday, Odd would return to helping the animals at the shelter, and everything would be fine.

"So . . . is something going to happen?" Jeremy asked.

"We're waiting," Odd told him.

They waited.

"How about now?" he asked.

"Still waiting," Odd said.

This is my fault, Even thought. Coming here had seemed like such a good plan, the kind of decisive thing that a hero would do. Getting trapped here, though . . . A real hero would have anticipated that. She wished Mom were here. She'd know what— "Mom! She's here in the magic world! We could find her!"

"Except we don't know where she is," Odd said.

Even sank down into the grass as she realized Odd was right. "And we don't have any way to contact her." Sure, this world was the source of all magic, and that was wonderful. But it wasn't what they needed right now.

Mom had a lot of meetings lined up in various territories so she could reach as many potential customers as possible, but she'd never said where they were. She could be anywhere. Hundreds of miles away. Or in the very next town. Dad had her itinerary, of course, but Dad wasn't here. They had no way of knowing where she was, and, even if they had known, they had no way to reach her. It wasn't as if mundane cell phones worked in the magic world, not that Even had one tucked in her fur anyway.

"If we can't contact Mom, then we have to get back to Dad on our own." Even spoke slowly, knowing that Odd wasn't going to like what she was thinking. "We have two choices: stay here and hope this gateway opens . . . or find a different gateway that *is* open."

"This is the only one that leads home," Odd protested.

"The others lead to someplace on Earth," Even said. "So long as we find one to go through, we can go to the nearest border store and ask them to call Dad." She tried to make this sound as if it were no big deal, though she dreaded that phone call. Dad was *not* going to be happy with them. "Dad will come get us wherever we end up."

"Unless it's Australia. Or Japan. Or the Arctic," Odd said, but she stopped, clearly considering it. "But at least we'd be in the right world, and you're right that there would be a border store nearby — there always is. They would help us get home."

"So what do you think?" Even asked. "Do we stay, or do we search?" She didn't know which was the right choice.

Odd shook her head. "The other gateways could be miles away. How do we even find them? And what if *they're* closed too? Or in a dangerous area? No, it's too risky. Girl Scout rule number one: if you get lost, you stay in one place so that people can find you. We should stay put and wait for the gateway to reopen."

"What if the other gateways close while we're waiting?" Even asked. "What if this is our chance and if we don't go now, we won't get home at all?"

"You don't know that that's a possibility," Odd said accusingly. "You just want to explore. You're using this as an excuse. I think you're *happy* we're stuck here!"

Even opened her mouth to object. She wasn't happy! They were cut off from home! Of course, she'd been excited to see the magic world—she'd only asked Mom a billion times if she could come with her to visit their former home—but that was before the gateway had closed behind them. "How can you think I'd be happy about this?"

"Because I *know* you. You want to be here!"

"When I'm eighteen and fully trained and prepared. Not now. Not like this." Yes, she had always wanted to see a giant stride across the landscape. She wanted to witness a wizard calling a thunderstorm out of the sky. She wanted to watch a herd of centaurs gallop freely across a valley and to see phoenixes burn in the sky as the sun set and to taste an enchanted river and to hear a mermaid sing and to touch a dragon's scales. *But I never wanted* this *to happen!*

"Fine. Sorry," Odd said. "So what do we do?"

Even had no idea if other gateways were having problems or if it was just this one. They had very little information at all. "We need to find out if other gateways are open and where they are. Maybe we can find someone to ask?"

"You can ask my parents," Jeremy said behind them.

Even gave a little jump. She'd been so focused on the vanished gateway that she'd forgotten he was still there.

"My family has a magic mirror," he said. "We can use it to find out about the other gateways — where they are, where they lead, and if they're open."

"Your family would help us?" Odd asked.

"Absolutely," Jeremy said, "and you know I can't lie. Ooh, but *you* can lie! Can you tell my parents that I found you here and offered to bring you to my family for their help, and you gave me the soda and Farmcats cards as a thank-you? That way I won't even have to hide my loot. It's a perfect solution!"

"Kind of think finding a way home is more important than soda, especially since he's not even un-cursing anything," Odd muttered to Even. "Just wants to drink it."

Jeremy heard her. "You know what they say: don't look a gift unicorn in the mouth. Do you want my help or not?"

"Absolutely," Even said. "Thank you."

"Sorry," Odd said. "We'd love your help."

Shaking his mane majestically, he reared back on his hind hooves. "Follow me!"

The sisters followed him. Glancing back at where the gateway was supposed to be, Even hoped they were making the right choice.

8

"IT'S NOT FAR," Jeremy said as he trotted toward the road. His tail swatted away a flower fairy as if it were a fly. Even and Odd hurried after him.

Even wished she'd been home during the brief moment the gateway was open. Dad could have transformed her back into herself, and then she wouldn't be waddling on short, stubby, furry legs, trying to keep up. No, that wasn't her wish. She wished they hadn't followed Jeremy to the bagel store at all, and she especially wished she hadn't had the bright idea to test the gateway.

This is all my fault.

But I'm going to make up for it. I'm going to get us to the unicorns, and they're going to help us find our way home. Of course, it would be easier to feel like she was leading the way if she weren't scurrying behind. "How far is 'not far'?"

"Just beyond the witch's house."

"A witch?" Odd asked. "What kind of witch? Evil fairy-tale witch, or friendly helpful witch? Is she going to keep us from reaching your family?"

"Oh no, she's nice," Jeremy said. "A witch is just a name for a magic user without a medallion. You know, not affiliated with the Academy of Magic."

"You can be a magic user without a medallion?" Even asked. She'd thought it was required by the Academy. They oversaw all magic use in Firoth, to ensure no one used it for evil purposes. And if you *did* use it for evil, they sent a hero, one of their wizards, to stop you.

"Sure, you can use magic without a medallion," Jeremy said. "The witch always said she meant to get one, but there was too much paperwork."

What was he talking about? He made getting a medallion sound as dull as paying a parking ticket, a long and tedious errand she'd gone on once with Dad.

"You'll see the hill soon," Jeremy continued, blithely unaware of Even's reaction. "We live both on it and in it. The dwarves built us caves for shelter from the rain, modeled after their underground palaces. I have my own cave room with Farmcats posters on all the walls. I'll show it to you!"

Even was so intent on looking ahead of them, trying to see the witch's house and the unicorns' hill beyond it, that when they suddenly reached a road, she stumbled over the bricks. She got her paws underneath her again and shook out her fur. Only then did she notice that the road was made of yellow bricks. The bricks were crumbling, laced with moss, and coated in a slimy lichen, but they were undeniably yellow.

For an instant, seeing the road, she forgot about her rush to reach the unicorns, her worry about being on the wrong side of the border, and everything. "Whoa, yellow brick road! Does it lead to the Emerald City?"

"What?" Jeremy asked.

"Like in *The Wizard of Oz*. It's a movie. And a book." She'd heard there was a history of magical immigrants influencing mundane artists, or becoming writers and artists and actors themselves. "There's a rumor that the author may have been from Firoth. In fact, there are a lot of famous people in our world who came from here. Actors and actresses, mostly. There used to be some Olympic athletes who were part troll. Really strong. But they can't do it now because of the blood testing."

"I literally don't understand half the words you just said," Jeremy complained.

Prodded by Odd, Even started walking again. As they continued, Odd tried to explain what the Olympics were. Before she could get very far, though, Jeremy gasped. "My hill!"

Even looked ahead but didn't see any hills.

Maybe I'm too short to see it, she thought. She considered asking Odd to lift her up, but that seemed way too embarrassing.

Jeremy broke into a gallop. His hooves sounded like bells ringing as they hit the yellow brick road. Odd ran after him, and Even tried to keep up, but with her skunk legs, the best she could do was an enthusiastic waddle. She arrived a few minutes later, panting, at the edge of a lake.

The lake glistened darkly. It was opaque, and its ripples held the same bright sea-blue as the sky. The western shore was obscured by the border mist, which swirled silently, licking at the water with bits of fog.

Tossing his mane and snorting, Jeremy paced back and forth on the shore. "It should be here! Our hill. Our flowers. Our clover. Our caves. Our home! It was here when I left!"

"Your home flooded?" Even asked.

She'd seen photos in the news of flooded areas, though, and this didn't look like that. No roofs half-submerged in water. No trees sticking up out of the water. This lake had a shore with rocks and sand and driftwood, as if it had been here for years. It certainly didn't look like an underwater hill.

"Are you sure this is the right spot?" Odd asked.

He let out a panicky neigh as he raced back and forth on the shore. "Of course I am! I've been on that road countless times. Over there, those are the trees that are supposed to be next to Unicorn Hill. And there's the witch's house, exactly where it always is. But no hill!"

Splash!

Using her tail for balance, Even rose up onto her hind legs and looked out over to the water. She saw a swirl of waves a few yards off from shore and a flash of an orange fish tail.

Slowing, Jeremy said, with disgust in his voice, "Mermaids."

"Really?" Even had never seen one, at least not that she could remember, and certainly not since they'd left Firoth. You couldn't swim across the border, or at least you couldn't if you used a gateway that opened into a bagel-store parking lot, so there had never been one in her family's shop. If the situation were different, she would have asked Jeremy a dozen questions about them. As it was . . .

"Maybe they know what happened," Odd suggested.

Shouting across the water, Even called, "Hello? Can you help us, please?"

"I don't think they'll help," Jeremy warned.

Odd waved. "Over here! Hi!"

A woman's head popped out of the water. She swam toward them, leaping like a dolphin, and Even saw her tail as she arched above the water. *Wow!* Even thought. *A mermaid!* For a second she nearly forgot she was stuck as a skunk, trapped on the wrong side of the border. She'd always wanted to see a mermaid.

Closer to shore, the mermaid slowed, swam in a circle, and opened her mouth to speak.

Even leaned toward the water, eager to hear what she was about to say. In Greek myths, mermaid-like sirens lured sailors to their death with the beauty of their voices. A real mermaid should sound like—

"Eeeeeeeeeeeeeeeee-iiiiiii-eeeeeeee!"

Odd clapped her hands over her ears. Sitting back, Even covered her ears with her paws. The shrill, glass-breaking squeal echoed across the lake, and a second mermaid swam closer and began to wail too. Her voice sounded like the squeak of Styrofoam but much, much louder.

"See?" Jeremy had to shout to be heard over the shrieks. "Not helpful!"

Even tried again, raising her voice as loud as she could. "Do any of you know where the unicorns are? Uni-corns. Like him. Horse with pointy horn. They're supposed to help us get home, or at least we hope they will, if we can find them. They used to live here."

Six mermaids squealed together, *"Eee-iiiiiii-eeeeeeey!"*

Even winced as they hit a particularly high note. "I think they're trying to tell us something?" Maybe it was a warning? Or an explanation? Or, ooh, a prophecy?

A gruff voice behind them said, "They're trying to say they want fish. Never met a mermaid before? Forget the stories. They're much more fish than person." A short, green-skinned man with a full bright-emerald beard waddled past them, hauling a bucket. He pulled a fish out of the bucket and tossed it toward the mermaids. "Poor creatures are starving to death!"

Shrieking, the mermaids fell on the fish like ducks on a piece of bread, if ducks sounded as though police whistles had been shoved down their windpipes.

"Sir, do you know where the unicorns have gone?" Even asked the green man.

"Don't know. Don't care." He tossed another fish. "If they're the ones who caused this, then good riddance to them."

"They were here," Jeremy insisted. "This was my home!"

Another fish. "If you're responsible, then you're the worst too."

"Responsible for what?" Jeremy shifted from hoof to hoof, shaking his mane. "What happened to Unicorn Hill? And who are you?"

Whispering, Odd asked Even, "And *what* is he?"

He heard her. "I'm a goblin. My name's Joj. And as to your hill . . . You really don't know? Huh. I'm the Academy-appointed caretaker in charge of this school of mermaids. I was doing my daily rounds, checking on the health of their scales and all that, when, *whoomp*, the lake up and moved here. Fine. Whatever. Except"—his voice rose higher and louder—"they're cut off from their river. The river that leads to the ocean! You know, the ocean with lots and lots of fish that *keeps them from starving to death!*" His green face was now tinted purple. "Do you have any idea how much fish a school of mermaids needs to survive? And how much gold it costs to buy enough fish to keep them happy?"

Even didn't, but he didn't give any of them a chance to answer.

"A lot. That's the answer. A lot of fish, and a lot of gold!" He dumped the rest of the fish from his bucket into the lake and then stomped back past them, as if the conversation were over.

"Is this a normal thing here?" Odd asked. "Lakes and hills just . . . move?"

"Does it seem normal?" the goblin snapped over his shoulder. "No!"

Fur bristling, Even stepped in front of Odd. "Don't yell at my sister. We don't know what's ordinary for you." Given where they were, all sorts of things could be possible.

Jeremy trotted after Joj. "Do you know where my home went?"

"Told you already," the goblin said. "No. And if you can't help, you can go away. I've got a lot of work to do to keep my mermaids from dying, thanks to whoever did this."

"But my family is supposed to be here! My mother, my father! I have aunts and uncles and cousins! Annoying, constantly underfoot cousins, but mine! They live here. With me. And sure, yes, maybe I often wished I didn't live here because it was boring and full of other unicorns, plus every time I went for a simple prance around a meadow, flower fairies would get stuck in my mane and sting my neck, but still, when you leave home, home isn't supposed to disappear!" His voice grew more and more panicked.

The sisters hurried after them, leaving behind the fish-chomping mermaids. Even tried to wrap her mind around the idea that a lake and a hill could move. Other than in an earth-quake, places were supposed to stay, well, in place. She'd never heard any stories or myths about land shuffling around on a whim. She *had* read about lost towns—Brigadoon, Shangri-La, Atlantis. And lakes could suddenly dry up. Or a lake could be created, if you dammed up a river. But *move?*

Grumbling to himself, Joj deposited the empty bucket outside a cottage that looked in danger of tumbling down—the walls were slats of wood hammered together askew, and the roof shingles looked like loose teeth about to fall out. As he reached for the door handle, the house rose into the air on enormous chicken legs, shifted to the left, and then settled down again, several feet away from Joj and his bucket. "I hate this place," Joj muttered.

"Is that the witch's house?" Even asked.

"Where is the witch who lives here?" Jeremy asked. "Does she know where my parents are? We have to find her! She may know what happened."

Picking up his bucket and moving it closer to the house again, Joj said, "The witch fled. Scared. Said it wasn't safe near the border anymore—border magic is all messed up, she said, and it's messing with the world. I'd flee too, except the mermaids don't have feet or wings. Can't leave them behind. I'm all that's keeping them alive."

"But what could scare a *witch?*" Odd asked.

The goblin flapped his arms, exasperated. "Haven't you been paying attention? Homes are disappearing and reappearing where they shouldn't be! The borderlands are unstable! That's more than enough to scare a witch. Or anyone with any sense."

Even asked Joj, "Have you contacted the Academy of Magic? Do they have an explanation? Or, even better, a solution?"

Joj snorted. "Don't you think that was the first thing I tried? Said they'll put me 'in the queue of complaints.' Humph." He tried again to open the door to the witch's house, and again the house sidled away from him.

"Where was your lake before?" Even asked. "Maybe it switched places with the hill?" She had no idea if geography could do that. Certainly she'd had no idea that mermaids squealed like irate dolphins.

For the first time, Joj looked more interested than mad. "Hmm, possible."

"Really? Because that was just a guess," Even said.

"My lake is supposed to be in a town called Lakeview . . ."

"Let's call it!" Jeremy said. "Maybe my family is there. Do you have a magic mirror?"

The goblin brightened to the point of almost smiling. "Yes!"

★★★

Joj didn't have his own mirror, but the missing witch did. After the chicken-legged house evaded Joj a few more times, Jeremy interrupted. "Excuse me, but I'm your neighbor. May I come in?"

The house immediately swung its door open.

"Sometimes you just have to ask," he said, with a hint of smugness.

The goblin grunted at him. "And sometimes your home up and moves no matter how polite you are."

Going inside felt like sticking your hand into a lunch bag left in a school backpack over the summer. The house smelled of mold and mildew, and everything looked moist. Even tiptoed across the sticky floor, careful not to let her fur brush against any of the decaying furniture.

"Why is it such a mess?" Even asked. "Is it because she's a witch?"

"It's because she's a slob," Joj said.

She wondered where the witch had gone when she'd fled, and she wished the witch had stayed to help. Joj and the mermaids clearly needed help, and so did Even, Odd, and Jeremy. *If I were a grownup with a medallion, and fully certified as a hero,* she thought, *maybe I'd know what to do. But I'm not, and I don't.* She hadn't realized how badly she'd been counting on the unicorns until now. She'd wanted to dump all of this into Jeremy's parents' laps. If unicorns had laps.

"Ta-da," Joj said, waving at a mirror. It was a tall standing mirror, with an ornate iron frame that was coated in cobwebs. "Did not have time to clean this place. For obvious reasons. Wish I could've gotten stuck with a witch who had better hygiene. No magic needed to dust once or twice a decade."

"Can we use it to call Dad?" Odd asked.

Even hadn't thought of that. It was a brilliant idea. "Maybe?"

Odd turned to Jeremy. "Can we try? And then you call your parents? Please?"

"I . . ."

"We'll be quick," Even promised. All it would take was a minute to tell Dad where they were and ask what to do; then Jeremy could make sure his family was okay.

"So long as I can make my call immediately after."

Odd knocked on the mirror frame, and dust flew up in a cloud. She coughed, waving her hand in front of her face to clear it away. "How do you make it call?"

"Don't hit it," Joj said. "Seven years bad luck if you break it."

Odd clasped her hands behind her back.

Even wondered if that was just a superstition here, like it was in the mundane world, or if the goblin was serious. She decided she wasn't going to test it, and she filed it away as yet another question to ask later, when they were safely home.

"Describe the mirror you want it to find," Joj said.

Even described the mirror in their parents' bedroom, and the goblin performed a series of taps around the frame of the mirror. "Mirror, mirror on the wall, here's the address you should call," he said.

"Lift me up," Even whispered, nudging against Odd. She didn't care about being embarrassed if she could see Dad.

Odd picked her up so she could see the mirror.

The glass fogged, a swirl of silvery gray. Even held her breath as she waited. She'd watched her parents use the magic mirror in their room, mostly to check on the news from Firoth, and she knew it always started with the fog. Soon an image would appear. She expected to be able to see into her parents' bedroom. Their mirror faced the bookshelf, in case of unexpected calls, and this one had to qualify as unexpected.

But no image appeared. It kept swirling.

"Are you sure you did it correctly?" Jeremy asked.

"Rude," Joj said. "Yes, I'm sure."

"Could you try it one more time?" Odd pleaded.

"The mirror can't get a message through because the border is closed," Even said as she realized the truth. She should have thought of that sooner. It was the same reason that Frank the centaur couldn't send his research back, the same reason she'd gotten stuck as a skunk yesterday, the same reason the fairy lights were out and the bagel shop was closed. Without an open gateway, magic of any kind couldn't penetrate the border.

By now, Dad must have started worrying about them—they'd been gone long enough that he'd expect them back. They had no way to tell him they were okay. Or not okay but not hurt. There was also no way to ask him for help. But maybe there were still people—or, more accurately, unicorns—who could help them out there somewhere . . . "Your turn," she said to Jeremy. "Try to call your family."

Even hopped out of Odd's arms onto a gingerbread table. Crumbs from the surface stuck to her paws. She jumped down to the floor and tried to wipe the crumbs off while Jeremy described his parents' mirror.

The goblin activated the mirror again, and the dark fog swirled. This time, though, it parted in the center. A white blob appeared. Jeremy pressed his muzzle against the glass. "Mama? Mama, can you hear me? It's me."

"Shimmerglow? Baby, is that you?" Her voice vibrated out of the mirror.

"Ahh! Don't call me that! I am not a baby anymore." But his voice was full of relief.

Rubbing against Odd's ankle, Even caught her attention and whispered, "Shimmerglow?" That was a much more awesome name for a unicorn than Jeremy.

Odd murmured back, "I see why he changed it."

Jeremy continued, huffing at the mirror as if that would make the fog clear. "Yes, Mama, it's me. I'm home. Except home isn't here. Where are you?"

"One second, our hill and everyone on it was where it's always been, and then, without warning, we were elsewhere. We were so worried when you didn't appear with us! Where have you been? Everyone was transported except you." Her voice sounded as if it was floating in the air around them. It was a musical voice, exactly the kind Even had always thought a unicorn should have. She scooted closer to the mirror for a better view, squeezing herself between Jeremy's hooves, but the mirror was still hazy.

"I didn't mean to worry you," Jeremy said, neatly avoiding answering the question. "Is everyone all right? There's a lake where Unicorn Hill is supposed to be. What happened? What do you mean 'transported'? Was it wizards? Witches? A spell gone wrong? A curse gone right? Or maybe—"

"We don't know," Jeremy's mother said, interrupting him gently. "We've heard reports of similar displacement problems all along the border, of both land and people, but as of yet we've heard no explanations." The fog was beginning to part, and they could see the face of a unicorn. Her eyes were bluer than the sky in either world, and she had golden lashes and a golden mane to match her golden spiral horn. Even could immediately tell she was older than Jeremy. *She looks wise,* Even thought. *And majestic. And one hundred percent unicornish.* "Who are you with, darling?" the unicorn asked.

Jeremy introduced the goblin first. "This is Joj. He's helping us use the witch's mirror to contact you. He was transported here with a lake filled with mermaids."

Joj stuck his face next to Jeremy's. He peered into the mirror, scowling at the hazy view. "I'm not supposed to be here. Are you in my home? Is that Lakeview? You better not be messing up my home. I want it back."

In a soothing voice, Jeremy's mother said, "We are as much victims as you are, and as much in the dark as to the cause of our unwelcome relocation. If our hill and caves had not moved with us, we would have already returned."

"And these are my new friends, Odd and Even," Jeremy continued. "They came through the gateway, and it closed behind them. They're looking for a way home."

"Oh, the poor dears!"

Even rose on her hind paws and waved hello with one of her front paws.

"Ask her about other gateways," Odd whispered.

"Mama, do you know if any of the gateways are working?"

The fog swirled around her face again, and Jeremy's mother appeared to retreat. Her voice sounded distant, and the words melded together. She pressed closer, her nostrils filling most of the mirror. "The one here is working. At least for now. It has been flickering off and on, which is unusual behavior for a gateway that has stood open for all recorded time. Several of the nearby residents are especially concerned because they have family across the border."

"Please, could you tell us where it is?" Odd asked.

"Head south along the border for fifteen miles, and you'll reach us," Jeremy's mother said. "We're near a border town called Lakeview, except there's no lake here."

Joj grumbled, "That's because the lake is *here*. With my mermaids."

"Hopefully, this will all be sorted out soon, and everything and everyone will return back to normal," Jeremy's mother said. As melodious as her voice was, she also sounded worried. Even's skin prickled under her fur. Did Jeremy's parents know if it was possible to return things to normal? Or was his mother just being optimistic? Hoping wasn't the same as lying.

"Better be," Joj said.

Of course it will be, Even thought, fiercely squashing any doubt. Now that she and Odd knew where to find Jeremy's parents . . . all they had to do was get there.

Leaning, Jeremy nudged Odd.

"Oh! Um. We've given Jeremy soda and Farmcats trading cards to thank him for his help." Odd's voice was stiff, but Jeremy's mother seemed to accept it as the truth.

"Very kind of you," she said. "I'm sure whatever 'soda' is, he appreciates it. In return, Shimmerglow, I think it would be very kind of you to help your new friends come to this gateway before it closes. Especially since you should be here with your family anyway. Families need to stick together in times like these."

"I'll help them," he promised.

"Come as fast as you can. I can't predict how long the gateway will stay open. No parent should have to suffer through the worry of a missing child." The look she gave Jeremy was pointed.

Jeremy hung his head low. "Sorry, Mama. We'll hurry."

9

"YOU CAN RIDE me," Jeremy offered, trotting out of the witch's house.

Odd's face lit up. "I know how to ride. I've done the pony ride at the apple orchard every single fall since we moved to Connecticut."

"You can ride me *if* you don't call me a pony." He tossed his magnificent mane to emphasize his point.

"Sorry," Odd said. She still looked delighted at the idea of riding him. It was nice to see her excited about something in this world. *It's my fault she's stuck here,* Even thought. *I thought I could help, but instead I made things worse.* She shouldn't have embarked on a quest before she was ready, even a quest as minor as a trip to the bagel store. At least they were on their way now to people —unicorns—who would know what to do.

Odd lifted Even up onto Jeremy's back and then pulled herself up behind Even.

Coming out of the witch's house, the goblin gave Odd a few fish-smelling jam sandwiches for their journey, as well as a bottle filled with (unenchanted, he assured them) water. When they tried to thank him, he waved off their words, saying he liked feeding people. He then wished them luck and hurried back to the lake to care for his mermaids.

Jeremy set off at a trot down the yellow brick road.

In the distance, they heard the mermaids shriek and squeal. The caterwauling faded the farther away they got. "How long do you think this will take?" Odd asked. "How fast do you think we're going? Twenty miles an hour? Thirty? Less? More?"

"I don't know," Jeremy said. "Not as fast as a car. Not as slow as a pony." He added a disgusted neigh after the word "pony."

"What if we're not fast enough?" Odd asked.

It was a worry that crept into Even's mind and caused her stomach to knot. What if the gateway closed before they got there? What if they couldn't go home?

Stop it, she told herself.

They were doing everything they could to get to the gateway and Jeremy's family as quickly as possible, and worrying about it wouldn't make them go one bit faster. She should do what Mom always said to do when they were anxious and think of five things she was grateful for.

One, they had a plan.

Two, they knew where they were going.

Three, they didn't have to walk.

Four, it wasn't raining or snowing or sleeting or tornado-ing.

Five . . .

"Wish we could just drive there," Odd said.

"What does it feel like to ride in a car?" Jeremy asked dreamily.

"It feels like you're inside a big can with windows, moving on a road," Even said. "It's not like this, with the wind in your face and fur." She lifted up her face to breathe in the cinnamon-sugar air. It ruffled her fur, massaging her cheeks. It felt and smelled wonderful.

The fifth thing I'm grateful for is the chance to breathe the air of Firoth, she thought. And see the sky of Firoth. And hear the distant song of magical birds. And know that soon the unicorns would help them cross the border, and they'd be back with Dad.

"No bugs in my eyes," Jeremy said. "No pain in my hooves. Have you ever flown in a helicopter?" He pronounced the word slowly, as if he'd never said it out loud before.

"Never," Odd said. "But I want to."

"You do?" Even twisted to look up at Odd. "Why? You can fly on your own every odd day. Or you could, if you practiced. Why would you care about flying in a helicopter?"

"Because they're cool," Jeremy answered for her.

"Why do you like mundane-world stuff so much?" Even

asked him. "Farmcats cards. Soda. Helicopters. You're a unicorn! Isn't that cool enough?"

Jeremy didn't answer for so long that Even began to think she'd insulted him. She hadn't meant to. She was honestly curious. He was nothing like what she'd expected a unicorn to be like. Except for having a shiny horn.

Odd nudged her and whispered, "I think you hurt his feelings."

"Jeremy, I'm sorry. I didn't mean —"

"It's not . . . It's just . . . I *know* I'm a unicorn, and that's awesome," Jeremy said. Pausing, he posed, as if to show off his unicorn-ness, and then continued. "I just don't want to be a unicorn *here*. Here, I'm just Shimmerglow — the unicorn kid who panics too easily and babbles too much. There . . . where you come from . . . I don't know. I'd be different. Better."

Even could understand wanting to be better — after all, that was the whole reason she practiced so much — but she didn't see what Farmcats and soda had to do with being braver or less panicky or whatever it was he wanted to be. "Can't you be better here?"

"Unlikely. It hasn't happened yet."

Even tried to think of the right thing to say to reassure him.

Odd spoke up. "I think you're fine the way you are."

He snorted. "Thanks." But it was clear he didn't believe her, and there wasn't much more either of them could think to say to that.

After a couple more miles of riding, they stopped by a field of red and yellow flowers to eat the lunch the goblin had given them. Odd dismounted and unwrapped the sandwiches, then laid one on the ground for Even. Sitting next to it, Even tried to lift the sandwich with her paws, but they didn't work quite the same way hands did. She ended up chasing the bread, slices of vaguely fish-smelling cheese, and gobs of jam around on the wrapper until finally she gave up and stuck her snout in.

She was chewing her way through the sandwich when the dragon appeared.

There was no hint that it was coming. Even heard a *pop* like a balloon, and the empty sky was suddenly filled by a very large, very upset dragon. Odd shrieked. Even jumped several inches into the air, and her tail lifted into spraying position. Rearing onto his hind legs, Jeremy pawed the air with his front hooves and neighed in alarm.

She'd imagined seeing a dragon hundreds of times. She'd seen plenty of CGI dragons in movies. She'd pored over illustrations made by artists who might or might not have been to Firoth. None of that had prepared her for the sight of a real dragon.

It was utterly massive, with outstretched wings that blocked the sun. Bright red, it was covered in scales that gleamed like metal, with feather-like strands that dangled from its neck. Screaming a guttural cry, it exposed swordlike teeth.

In a voice that sounded like a school fire alarm, the dragon shrieked, "Where are my children? What have you done with them?"

"We haven't done anything!" Odd cried.

"They were with me!" the dragon yelled in a voice so loud that it made Even's skunk ears ache. "And now they are not! You took them from me!"

"We didn't!" Even shouted. "You just appeared!"

"Then filthy wizards took me from them! Are you the minions of filthy wizards? You must be. You're here, and my children are not!" The dragon's neck began to glow brighter and brighter, like a fire had been lit beneath its red scales . . . *Oh no,* Even thought.

She spun around and bounded through the grass. "Run!"

Jeremy bolted.

"With us!" Even shouted after him.

"Sorry!" He circled back to them. "Very sorry."

Odd scooped up Even by the scruff of her neck and climbed onto Jeremy's back. As soon as they were on him, he galloped away from the dragon.

"You're going back the way we came!" Odd shouted. "You're going the wrong way!"

"Away from the angry dragon is always the right way!" he shouted back.

Even clung to Odd's shirt with her claws. Over Odd's shoulder, she saw the dragon, red scales bright against the blue-green sky. It pumped its wings, and the wind bent trees sideways.

"She's right!" Even called. "It'll catch us this way! There's no place to hide!"

"What do we do?" Jeremy asked. "I don't want to be eaten by a dragon! Or roasted by a dragon! Or torn to pieces by a—"

Even scanned the horizon. Off in the distance, across a field of flower fairies, she saw purple boulders sparkling as bright as amethysts. "There!" She pointed with her paw and then clung to Odd again. "See the purple rocks? Go that way!"

He shifted direction, racing across the meadow. Fairies flew up around them, and Odd batted them away. "Ow!" she cried as they bit her.

Even bared her fanglike skunk teeth and hissed at them. She waved her tail menacingly, as best she could while still clinging to Odd's shirt.

Swooping down, the dragon breathed fire, and the flames danced across the meadow. More flower fairies took to the air, shrieking as they fled. Jeremy aimed for the labyrinth of boulders.

"Faster!" Even yelled.

"I'm already going faster!" Jeremy panted. "I told you . . . I am *not* . . . good under pressure! I do *not* like this at all!"

"Duck, Odd!" Even shouted. She scrambled up onto Odd's back, stuck her tail in the air, and sprayed as hard as she could behind them as the dragon dove, skimming the fiery meadow.

The spray hit the dragon's mouth as it opened its jaws to breathe more fire. Coughing, it flew upward, away from them. Jeremy raced in between the boulders.

"Watch out!" Odd shouted.

He leaped over a rock and then ducked beneath an arch.

They zigzagged through a maze of purple stone while the dragon chased them overhead—the gaps between the rocks were too narrow for it to reach them and too deep for the dragon's fire to touch them, but the dragon was persistent. Shadows crossed them as the dragon soared above, and they felt heat from the flames as the fire scoured the top of the maze.

Up ahead, Even spotted an alcove. "Hide there!"

Jeremy raced for it, jumping over rocks and skirting around stone pillars, and then plunged into the alcove. An overhang of purple stone blocked the sky—and the dragon. Jeremy stopped, his sides heaving. Odd and Even clung to his back. All of them held quiet.

Overhead, they heard the dragon cry. Its wing beats sounded like a windstorm. *Stay quiet,* Even thought. *Stay calm.* The rock walls were high. The dragon couldn't reach them here.

Gradually, the sound of wing beats subsided.

"Don't move," Even whispered.

The dragon returned twice more. Keeping as still as possible, they stayed hidden and silent until all was quiet. At last, Even said, "I think it gave up."

Carefully, Jeremy stepped out of the alcove. They all looked up, but saw only blue sky peeking between the rock walls. Odd slid off his back. She lifted Even down and set her on a rock, and then she plopped onto the mossy ground.

"You were amazing," Odd told Jeremy. "I think you ran faster than a car."

"Really? I didn't think I could do it, but I did it!" Jeremy paused and ducked his head as if embarrassed. "We're going to forget about how I initially ran away, right?"

Even grinned. "Already forgotten."

They waited for a while longer, until they felt certain it was safe to move on.

After picking their way out through the stone maze, they crossed the meadow and returned to the yellow brick road. They all checked the sky frequently as they continued on. "Do you think that's going to happen again?" Odd asked.

"It shouldn't have happened at all," Jeremy said. "Dragons don't live in this part of the world. Their home is far to the west, hundreds of miles from here, and the Academy of Magic has treaties with them to keep them in their own territories. I've never even seen one before. Truthfully, I thought they could have been mythical."

"*You* thought *they* . . ." Even shook her skunk head. "Never mind."

"Well, that dragon was not happy to be here," Odd said, in the understatement of the year.

"It did seem surprised." Even thought back to the popping sound she'd heard. It had appeared out of nowhere. "Can dragons teleport?"

"They can't," Jeremy said.

"Maybe whatever caused the unicorns and mermaids to vanish and reappear also caused the dragon to appear here," Even said.

They all thought about that. It was an alarming idea.

"Maybe we should hurry," Even suggested.

"Agreed," Jeremy said. "Really don't want to face *more* dragons. Or werewolves. Or gorgons. Or basilisks. Or—"

"How about instead of worrying about it," Even said, "we just run?"

Leaving the site of the dragon attack behind them, Jeremy galloped toward Lakeview.

★★★

By the time they reached a sign welcoming them to the border town of Lakeview, Jeremy's sides were damp with sweat. Even felt cramped in muscles she wasn't sure she was supposed to have, even as a skunk. They'd lost a lot of time to hiding from the dragon, but at last they'd made it! *This is it!* she thought. *We're finally going home! We did it!*

Perking up, Jeremy cheered, "It's here!"

"What is?" Odd asked.

"Home!" He picked up his pace.

Ahead, the road looked broken, with bricks jumbled together at the foot of a hill, as if the yellow brick road had been bull-dozed. Halfway up the slope, she saw the silhouettes of several unicorns standing beside a shadow that looked like an opening to a cave.

Even couldn't see beyond the hill, but the border—and, more important, the gateway—had to be on the other side. Just a few more minutes and they'd be back where they belonged. Or at least they'd be in the right world. They'd contact Dad from the nearest border store, and he'd know what to do and how to get both them and Mom home.

Despite being unprepared, we didn't do half bad, she thought. Then she considered the fact that they weren't supposed to be here at all. *Or at least it could have been worse,* she amended.

"Mama!" Jeremy called.

One of the unicorns broke away from the others and gal-loped down the hill toward them. Her mane flowed in the wind, her horn sparkled in the sun, and when she whinnied, it sounded like music. Now this . . . *this* was a unicorn like Even had imagined! Majestic! Glorious! The mirror hadn't done her justice. *This* was a unicorn who could solve problems, grant wishes, and send them home!

Jeremy ran toward his mother. Reaching her, he skidded to a stop.

Odd, holding Even, climbed off his back. Squirming in Odd's arms, Even twisted to get a better look at the magnificent full-grown unicorn.

Dipping her head down to his, Jeremy's mother nuzzled his face with hers. "My baby, my darling, my sweet little sugar plum!" *Not just glorious,* Even thought. *Loving, too.* She was everything a unicorn should be.

Jeremy rubbed his cheek against hers and then seemed to remember they had an audience. "Gah! Not a baby. Don't cuddle me in front of my friends, Mama."

She quit nuzzling but only backed a few inches away. "When we realized you hadn't come with us, we tried to find you! Uncle Sunflower went to look for you. We began to worry you'd crossed the border. With all the uncertainty lately—"

"I came to find you," Jeremy said, "as soon as I could. But Mama . . . what happened?"

"Sweetheart . . . don't be upset, but you need to know that when the hill moved, it shook everything. Several of the caves collapsed." Though she was delivering bad news, her voice was still beautifully musical.

"Is everyone okay? How many caves? A lot of them? *My* cave? Is my cave okay?"

"We got everyone out of the caves in time," she reassured him.

Even felt the warmth of the unicorn's voice roll blissfully over her, before she noticed that Jeremy's mother hadn't answered the question about his cave. *Unicorns can't lie,* she thought. *But they can omit.* She immediately wished she hadn't had that thought.

"But . . . but . . ."

His mother nuzzled his face again. "You're back, and everyone is all right. And that's what's important."

Even couldn't help but wonder what else Jeremy's mother wasn't saying. *Stop it,* she told herself. *We made it here. That's all we had to do. Our adventure is over. The grownups will take charge now.*

"But—"

"How about you introduce me to your new friends?" she suggested. "I'm Starry Delight. Please, call me Starry. So very lovely to meet you. I am sorry that we aren't greeting you under better circumstances. Did you have any problems along the way?"

"A dragon appeared, out of nowhere," Jeremy said.

Starry gasped. "But there aren't supposed to be dragons anywhere near here!"

"I think the dragon agreed with that," Odd said. "It seemed surprised too. And unhappy. We really want to get home before anything else happens. Can you help us? Please?"

A few other unicorns had joined them, and they were all regarding the sisters with what looked like pity. Even felt a growing unease, a knot returning to the pit of her stomach. *What if . . . We can't be too late. It has to be open!* She pushed the feeling away. "It's still open, isn't it?"

The unicorns looked at one another, and Even knew the truth before Starry Delight spoke. "I'm so very sorry, my dear. But the gateway closed shortly after you contacted us. It hasn't reopened."

Even felt her heart thumping faster in her chest. But . . . but the unicorns were supposed to send them home! *We made it here,* she thought. *That was supposed to be enough!*

"Then where's another gateway?" Odd asked.

"Why don't you come rest?" Starry suggested, as if Odd hadn't asked anything.

The knot of worry tightened even more. The unicorns dipped their heads in sympathy. Even felt her tail rising up, as if it sensed danger and instinctively wanted to spray.

"But . . . we need to go home," Odd said. "Please, you have to help us go home!"

"I am so terribly sorry, my dear children," Starry said sorrowfully. "I hate to be the bearer of bad news . . ."

Don't panic, Even told herself and her tail. *Maybe it isn't that bad. Maybe there's one open but it's far. Maybe this gateway will reopen soon. Maybe it's moved but we can still reach it!*

". . . but *all* the gateways are closed."

Even sprayed.

10

"ALL OF THEM?" Odd squeaked as the unicorns recoiled
from Even's scent.

Oh no, Even thought. Her tail flexed again as if it wanted to
spray more. *No, no, no, this isn't right at all!* She grasped at hope.
"We don't know what's wrong with them. They could reopen
any minute."

"That's right, little furry one, keep a positive attitude!"
Starry said encouragingly. She pranced sideways, positioning
herself upwind of Even. "All our problems could fix themselves
by dawn, and we could wake in delight to discover our home
is back where it belongs. In the meantime, eat, sleep, and enjoy
our hospitality . . . though I do apologize that, under the present
circumstances, we cannot offer more."

Eat and sleep? This wasn't how this was supposed to go at all.
"What if the gateway opens again and we're not near it?" Even

asked. "We need to be ready to go through it the second it starts working again."

It had to reopen, didn't it? It couldn't be closed forever.

She felt as if she were trapped in one of those awful fairy tales where you made a wish and it came true in the worst possible way. Yes, she'd always wanted to return to Firoth, but not like this.

"We promise we'll let you know the instant the gateway reopens," Starry said soothingly. "It's being watched—don't worry. You weren't the only ones affected by its closing, and our home's translocation wasn't the only side effect. Magic has been faulty all along the border. Geography has been shuffling around—homes moved and creatures displaced from their homes, like the dragon that you saw, and others. A flock of very confused pixies was just here as well. We believe the malfunctioning border magic is responsible for the appearance of so many creatures outside their normal territories."

"More dragons?" Odd yelped.

But Starry was already trotting up a slope that was littered with boulders and torn-up chunks of grass and flowers, and all she said was, "Come along, children."

Even weaved through the debris, trying to keep up with Odd and the unicorns. She hopped over a fallen branch and shook her tail free of the leaves. "What do you mean, 'malfunctioning'?" she called after Jeremy's mom.

"Is it why our home moved?" Jeremy asked.

"Yes, we believe it is," Starry said. "Our world is a special place, full of magic and wonder, but it's our connection to the mundane world that gives Firoth stability. Without that connection . . . The ramifications so far have only been seen on the border, but they will spread across the land if the gateways don't reopen. All of Firoth could become unstable, with all of our citizens—and geography—subject to translocation without warning, along with other effects." She then continued in a chipper voice, "But don't worry. I'm sure the magic simply needs to refuel itself."

"What do you mean by that?" Even asked. *Please, let there be an explanation!* She wanted to go back to believing it was all going to work out.

"Border magic is like all magic. You can picture it as water beneath the ground, filling a reservoir. Drain the lake, and you have to wait for it to fill back up before you can drink from it again. We believe that's what's happened with the magic that fuels the gateways. We have to wait for the border magic to, in essence, fill up again, like a wizard waits for his or her personal magic to refill, and then all the unsettling side effects should abate. I'm hopeful that will happen soon. In the meantime, we'd be delighted if you'd stay with us."

"We can't stay!" Odd cried. "We need to go home!"

Even echoed the sentiment. "She's right. We only meant to

check if the gateway was working. We didn't mean to stay in Firoth longer than a few minutes. There must be another way back to our world."

Trotting up the hill, Starry didn't seem to hear their protests. "I wish I could offer you your own cave for the night, but all our side tunnels either collapsed or are currently unstable. Until repairs can be made, we are all utilizing the Great Cave, but we will do our best to see that you're comfortable for however long you're with us."

She doesn't know how long that will be, Even realized. The unicorns had no clue why this was happening or how to fix it either. All the cheerfulness in the world couldn't hide the fact that Starry didn't know when the gateway was going to reopen. She'd said by morning it *could* be back to normal.

But what if it wasn't?

What if it didn't reopen? What if none of the gateways reopened?

It wasn't a lie that Starry was hopeful. They were all hopeful. But none of them *knew.*

Even hopped over the roots of another fallen tree. By the time they'd climbed up to the unicorn cave, her sides were heaving, and her tongue was hanging out the side of her mouth. She joined Odd as they followed their hosts inside.

For a brief second, she forgot about their situation and

marveled at the sparkle of the unicorn cave. It was like nothing she'd seen before. The word "cave" didn't fit what Even saw. She felt as if she were inside a jewelry box. The walls and the ceiling were flecked with hundreds, thousands, of gems: rubies, emeralds, diamonds. All of them sparkled and winked. She didn't know where the light was coming from — batteries? Magic? "It's amazing!" Even said.

"I feel like I've fallen into a princess-party supply bin," Odd said.

As a skunk, Even couldn't quite manage to roll her eyes the same way she could as a human, but she tried. "Doesn't anything impress you?"

"Being able to go home would impress me."

Louder, Even said so the unicorns could hear, "It's beautiful."

"It *was* beautiful," Starry said sadly.

Even tore her gaze from the glitter around her to notice that jewels littered the floor. Bits of wall had crumbled and lay in heaps of rubble. Dust-coated items, including books and satchels, were piled up in the shadows. The debris blocked what looked like tunnels leading away from the Great Cave.

Jeremy let out a cry and galloped across the cave. Rooting through a pile with his horn and hooves, he unearthed a torn Farmcats poster. His mother trotted after him and spoke in low tones.

"Poor Jeremy," Odd said.

"At least he's home," Even said.

"Sort of," Odd said. "He *is* with his family." They watched the two unicorns from across the cave. "Hey, I guess that's one thing I'm grateful for. I can't think of another four."

"I can't either," Even admitted.

Despite how far and fast they'd traveled, they'd failed to make it home today. Dad had given her her first quest—go to the gateway by the bagel store and report home—and so far she had failed spectacularly.

But soon she'd do better. She had to.

"Tomorrow," Even said, a promise to both herself and Odd. "We'll get home tomorrow."

"I hope you're right," Odd said.

So do I.

***

Once Jeremy was calmer, he and his mother returned. Starry brought a satchel with her, carrying the strap in her teeth, and laid it on top of a table-size boulder. "I believe this portion is suitable to your palates. Please eat. I know you've had a long journey."

Even wanted to say she wasn't hungry and it was more important to figure out another way home, but in truth, she *was* hungry. And she had no idea how to begin figuring out what to do next. Maybe if she ate, she'd have more ideas. She pawed at the rock. She didn't think skunks were climbers, but before she could find out for certain, Odd scooped her up and deposited her next to the food.

"Thanks," Even said, to both Starry and Odd.

Opening the bag, Odd took out a loaf of bread, a wedge of cheese, and a container of salad, as well as several cupcakes. Sniffing the cheese, Even avoided the cupcakes. Now that she'd met Jeremy, she knew she'd never look at a cupcake the same way again.

As they divvied up the food, Starry asked, "So I am to understand that your home is the mundane world? How did you come to be in our world at this inopportune time?"

Jeremy froze. His eyes were wide and worried.

Even wasn't going to get him in trouble, especially not after he had brought them all the way here *and* carried them away from an irate dragon. "We were testing the gateway, and we got stuck on the wrong side. Jeremy thought that you might be able to help us."

He gave her a slight, grateful nod.

"Forgive me for being nosy, but was your home always the mundane world?" Starry asked. She still sounded friendly and upbeat, and Even appreciated that. It let her pretend that everything was okay—they were just having a friendly conversation with a unicorn over dinner, and everything would be back to normal soon, including the unicorns' collapsed caves.

Even helped herself to a bit of carrot. It tasted more delicious to her as a skunk than it ever had when she was a human. She tried a bit of lettuce next. She hadn't realized how very hungry she'd gotten, with all the worrying and escaping from dragons they'd been doing. "We were born in this world, but we moved to the mundane world when we were little kids."

"It's home now," Odd added. "And I want to get back as soon as possible."

The lettuce tasted as sweet as cotton candy. *Maybe I should transform into a skunk the next time Mom insists I eat more veggies,* she thought. And then she couldn't help the little thought that popped up: *What if there isn't a next time?*

If the gateways didn't start working . . .

If the border stayed closed . . .

She wasn't going to think like this. She was going to hope that it all magically fixed itself by morning, like Starry had said. After all, magical things happened all the time here. Maybe the Academy had already sent a hero to fix the problem.

"Your parents must be very worried," Starry said. "Parents always worry about their children. It's universal, no matter what world you're from." She leveled another look at Jeremy, and he hung his head guiltily, even though it wasn't his fault that his home had been transported. Of course, it *had* been his fault that he wasn't with the other unicorns when it moved. "But I am curious why your family left Firoth when you so clearly belong here."

Even had wondered that many times herself, but maybe Starry was asking because Even was so furry? "I'm not really a talking skunk."

"She's usually a human girl," Odd explained. "She just got stuck like that because she can't work magic on odd days." She then glanced at Even and added, "But I think she makes a great talking-animal sidekick."

"Ha. Very funny." Flicking her tail, Even pretended to glare at her. At least Odd was back to joking. Maybe she wasn't busily imagining the worst. *Maybe I should stop imagining the worst too,* Even thought. *At least until the worst happens.* "I'll be back to human when I wake up tomorrow—it'll be an even day."

Starry was looking from one to the other of them and back again. "Your names are Even and Odd, and you work magic on even and odd days?"

After swallowing one more bite of lettuce, Even explained, "Well, some months have thirty-one days, so the even-and-odd thing doesn't always match the dates on the calendar—we just call them even and odd days because it's easier. Basically, we have magic on alternating days." This was the point where Even expected Starry to chuckle and say how clever their names were. That was what the border-shop customers always did when they learned about the sisters' "quirk" of alternating magic.

But to Even's surprise, Starry didn't laugh. Instead she said, "I've heard of you."

"You have?" Even asked.

"Do you know our mom, Janet Berry?" Odd asked eagerly.

Excellent question! Even thought. If Starry knew how to reach Mom—

"I'm afraid I haven't had the pleasure, but I have heard your family's story. Every once in a while, talk of you comes up— how splendid to see that you both are doing well!"

Even wasn't sure she'd call being stuck as a skunk and unable to get back home as "doing well."

"What do you mean, you've heard our family's story?" Odd asked. "What story?"

"The story of how your powers were split is taught by the Academy of Magic," Starry said, "as a warning about the dangers of experimental magic."

"Our powers weren't split," Odd said. "We were born this way."

"What experimental magic?" Even had no idea what Starry was talking about.

"Perhaps I've mixed you up with other children. I wouldn't want to spread false information. Unicorns, as you may or may not know, pride ourselves as the spreaders of truth."

"You mean we love to gossip," Jeremy said, mid-chew. He was halfway through eating a pile of clover. "I want to hear the story. I've never heard of people with split powers."

Odd insisted, "We were born this way."

"Are you twins?" Starry asked.

"Well, no," Odd said. "Even's a year older."

"And wiser," Even said.

"That's debatable," Odd said. "But what does being twins have to do with it? Were the kids you heard about twins?"

"The opposite," Starry said. "If you were twins, it would be understandable that your powers were shared in some way. Many twins are born with identical powers or complementary powers. Some even—" Cutting herself off, the unicorn studied their faces. "Could it be you were never told the truth?"

"What truth?" Odd asked.

"Your truth, of course," Starry said. "You, if you are indeed those sisters I heard about, weren't born with split magic. One of you was born with magic, and the other was born without."

It was such a simple statement: one of them was supposed to have magic and one wasn't. But it echoed inside Even. She felt her tail tense and firmly tucked it underneath her.

She saw that Odd was frozen, staring at Starry. The words had hit her, too.

One born with magic, and one without.

"It's common enough, even with parents who both have magical abilities," Starry said. "Everyone agrees that you were healthy and happy toddlers. Different destinies lay in front of you, of course, but that can be glorious in and of itself."

It explained so much. Even had always felt like she was

supposed to have magic, and Odd had always wished she didn't have any. *If I had been born fully magic* . . . "What happened?"

"Your parents were highly respected researchers, studying the essence of magical power itself. They were, with the blessing of the Academy of Magic, conducting experiments on a power stone."

"What's a power stone?" Even asked.

"It's a rare artifact that allows the manipulation of magic. Very poorly understood. Your parents were on the cutting edge of research, looking for ways to use the stone to siphon magic from the earth to create a stream of boundless power. If they'd succeeded, it could have meant the end to the daily limits that magic users face, and it could have made it possible for those without, or with lesser capacities, to use magic if they so wished. The Academy of Magic was very excited about the potential."

"What happened?" Odd asked.

"There was an accident," Starry said sadly. "During one of their experiments . . . Perhaps they failed to seal the laboratory properly or to account for the range of the stone. Regardless, unbeknownst to them, during one of their most innovative experiments, their beloved daughters wandered too close. Instead of taking magic from a natural *inanimate* source —such as the earth or the wind or the sea—the stone siphoned power from one sister and then shared it between them. As a result, the sisters were said to possess magic on alternating days. And thus they gained the nicknames Even and Odd."

She was never meant to have magic, Even thought. *I was.* It was a stunning thought, yet it also felt completely right. She'd always felt magical.

Why hadn't Mom and Dad told them?

"At last inquiry, I had heard that your parents had abandoned their careers as researchers and moved far away, but that was several years ago. I hadn't heard an update on your story since. Have you been well?"

"Fine," Odd said faintly.

"Amazing!" Starry was beaming at both of them, clearly unaware of how shocked the sisters were. "Everyone assumed the effects would be catastrophic to your lives."

It was supposed to be mine, Even thought.

And their parents had never told them.

"What a remarkable opportunity to share a story with the very people that story is about!" Starry gushed. "Enjoy the rest of your dinner. I'll check on the gateway and will let you know if there is any news. When you're finished, Jeremy will help you find blankets and show you where you can sleep."

"Thanks," Even said, speaking just as faintly as Odd had.

Both of them stared at Jeremy's mother as she walked across the cave, her hooves ringing like chimes on the obsidian floor.

She'd just delivered the truth about their past as cheerfully as if she had told them about sunny weather.

Odd's face squinched up. Looking at her, Even laid a paw on her arm. She couldn't tell how Odd was taking the news. Was she upset? Mom and Dad had lied about their origin story for all these years. They'd never even mentioned being researchers, much less causing an accident that had led to Even's and Odd's futures unfolding differently than they would have otherwise.

Odd began to laugh.

"Um, are you okay?" Even asked.

Odd lifted her up by the armpits. Even felt her whiskers twitch, and her tail swatted back and forth like a cat's. "Do you know what this means?" Odd asked, holding her so they were looking eye to eye.

"Mom and Dad aren't as good at magic as they think they are?" Even guessed. She tried to make her voice light, but it shook anyway. She could think of several things it meant: it was because of Mom and Dad that she wasn't fully magical, because of them that the family had had to move to the mundane world, because of them . . .

"It means it's not my fault," Odd said. "I'm bad at magic for a reason!"

"Yeah, you don't practice."

"It means there's a reason I'm the way I am. And a reason you're the way you are."

"Um, Odd, can you put me down?" Even wiggled her back paws in the air. It was completely undignified to be lifted up by one's little sister and held like the prize piglet at a county fair.

"We have to get home," Odd said, setting Even on the table. "Mom and Dad have a *lot* of explaining to do."

Even agreed with that one hundred percent.

11

'EVEN WOKE IN a corner of a bejeweled cave and blinked a few times before she remembered when and where she was. It was an even day. She was in Firoth. With Odd. And a lot of unicorns. Uncurling herself, she stretched out her tail — and froze.

I still have a tail.

Why do I still have a tail?

Forcing herself to calm down, she took a deep breath and concentrated. Carefully, she painted a picture of herself inside her imagination. She remembered what it was like to have hands with fingers, to have two legs that she walked on, to have hair on her head and no fur. She fixed that memory in her mind and pushed an image of her skunk self into it.

She felt herself tingle.

Yes! Please, yes!

The tingle spread all over her, and her fur vibrated. She

felt her legs begin to stretch. Her back lengthened, and her tail shrank until it disappeared.

A second later, Even was human, lying in a nest of blankets between piles of jewels. She hugged her arms. Arms! She'd missed having arms. And feet! Look at her feet, wearing her sneakers! She patted her hair, relieved it didn't feel like fur.

"Odd, I'm back!" She stood up, wobbled, and put her arms out until she remembered how to balance on two legs. "Wake up, Odd!" Nearby, a few unicorns stirred. Most of the unicorns were already awake and outside the cave. Even spun in a circle like she was on a fashion runway. "Who has two thumbs and knows how to use them? Me!"

"Is it open?" Odd asked, her eyes still closed.

"What?"

"The gateway," Odd said. "Can we go home?"

Even quit spinning. Oh. For a moment, she'd forgotten.

At least it was good news that she was human again, right?

But the fact that no one had woken them to say the gateway had reopened was bad news.

"I . . . don't know," Even said, subdued.

Odd didn't even slow to brush her fingers through her hair before marching out. Even hurried after her. Coming outside from the darkened cave, she shielded her eyes from the sudden light. As her eyes adjusted, she saw that Odd had already started making her way down the slope toward a stream at the base of Unicorn Hill. Several unicorns were drinking from it. As she hurried to catch up to her sister, she wondered if the stream was supposed to be connected to the mermaids' lake.

In the morning light, the hillside looked even worse than it had when they'd arrived. Whatever force had moved the unicorns' hill hadn't been gentle. It looked as if the earth had been pried up by the plump fingers of an oversize toddler and then dropped back down.

One unicorn broke from the herd. As Even watched it trot closer, she recognized Starry Delight. "Good morning, children! Ah, you must be Even, in your human form. I see the family resemblance now."

"Is the gateway open?" Odd asked without any preamble.

"Did you sleep well? I hope you had a comfortable night filled with delicious dreams!" Starry's voice was cheery, and Even wondered if she was dodging the question. Or maybe she was just naturally perky?

Odd said, "I had nightmares all night that the gateway didn't open and we were trapped here, and we never saw our home or our friends or our parents ever again. Please tell us. Did the gateway open? Did any of them open?"

The unicorn sighed, and Even guessed what she was going to say before she spoke. "I'm afraid not, my dear," Starry said, her voice full of sympathy.

"Are you sure?" Even asked. "They're closed? All of them? The one to New York City? Tokyo? The Antarctic research station? That one's not very popular except with Yetis, but I've heard about it."

"All closed."

"Fresno?"

"I don't know where that is, but closed," Starry said.

"It has a lot of fast food," Even said. "Really popular gateway. What about the ones to Europe? Those were heavily used a few hundred years ago, my parents said. They're more strictly regulated now, unlike ours."

"Please, we'll go anywhere we can get to," Odd begged. "So long as it's in the right world. From there we can get home. There must be a gateway open to somewhere!"

"She's right," Even said. "The gateways have always been open." She knew her history. Open gateways were the explanation for the Grimms' fairy tales, *Beowulf, Alice in Wonderland,* and those famous unicorn tapestries, as well as a few of the stranger cartoons that Mom and Dad liked from the 1980s. Their worlds had always been connected, at least as far as she knew. "What would make them all suddenly close?"

"We don't know, but we do know of an expert in the field, a wizard named Lady Vell. She has made a study of border magic, the wellspring of power that fuels the gateways. We are hoping she can provide some assistance."

"Great!" Even said. "Can we use your magic mirror to call her? Ask her to help us?"

"Unfortunately, we haven't been able to reach her yet," Starry said. "Either the problems with the border magic are affecting our mirror connection, or too many are trying to contact her at the same time. The border closing has caused chaos with the land and separated a great number of families, and I'm sure others have thought to turn to her too. Don't worry, though—we will keep trying to reach her. We only started yesterday. I feel certain we'll have success soon."

She had no way of knowing that. It occurred to Even that though she had to tell the truth, Starry Delight took optimism to an extreme. It made Even wonder if she should take what Starry said with a grain of salt.

Maybe we can't wait for the unicorns to fix things, Even thought. *Maybe we need this Lady Vell instead.* She might have the answers they needed. "What if we try to talk to her in person?" she asked. "Can we do that? Where does she live?"

"Would it make you feel better to try?" Starry asked.

It wasn't about feeling better, she wanted to say. It was about getting home. "Yes. Definitely yes," Even said instead. Beside her, Odd was nodding vigorously.

Raising her musical voice, Starry called across Unicorn Hill, "Spring? Effervescent Spring, could you come here a moment, please?"

A unicorn trotted across the hillside of torn-up flowers toward them. His mane was rainbow-colored, and his hide sparkled in the sunlight. Starry introduced him as Effervescent Spring, Jeremy's father. "These two are asking about Lady Vell, Spring," Starry said. "Do you know where her estate is?"

"Pleasure to meet you," Jeremy's father said in a deep voice, the baritone counterpart to Starry's lovely soprano. He sounded as if he were singing opera. "I have never spoken with Lady Vell myself, but I know her estate lies just north of the capital of Firoth, New City."

"Where's New City?" Even asked.

"Due north from our current location," he said. "A half-day ride. Perhaps you would be most comfortable traveling with a known companion? Shimmerglow, would you please join us?"

Extracting himself from the herd, Jeremy came over to them. He greeted his parents and then asked Even and Odd, "What is it? Are you going home? Is there another gateway open somewhere? Or is something new wrong? Is the hill going to move again? Last time my Farmcats poster got all bent up, and I guess there are worse things—okay, maybe a lot worse things. What happens to our home if it moves again? What if more caves collapse?"

"Shimmerglow," Starry said gently. "Hush."

"Or what if they don't collapse, but everything gets all mixed

up and no one knows what belongs to who?" He was still carrying his satchel, Even noticed. Given the cave-ins, he probably
wanted to keep his precious soda and Farmcats cards close.

"'Whom,'" Starry corrected. "And hush, Shimmerglow. Your
friends want to try to speak to Lady Vell, a wizard just north of
New City."

"Oh, I love New City!" Jeremy said, relief in his voice. He'd
clearly been expecting a new crisis, not another journey.

To Even and Odd, Starry said, "Shimmerglow has been
to the city many times and knows the way. You could make it
there and back by dinnertime, if you wish, but there is no guarantee she will speak with you. We can't send word that you're
coming, and she may be unwilling to receive guests she hasn't
invited. Wouldn't you rather stay here while we try to call her?
Our hospitality—"

"Thank you," Even said, "but we'd rather try than wait." She
glanced at Odd to make sure she agreed and saw that her sister
was already climbing onto Jeremy's back, ready to go.

***

It was, Even thought, *much* better riding a unicorn as a human
than as a skunk. For one thing, she had a nicer view. She could
actually see the road in front of them, instead of just Jeremy's
mane.

As Even, Odd, and Jeremy left Unicorn Hill (with instruc-
tions to return by nightfall for "a comfortable night's sleep with

delightful dreams") and rejoined the yellow brick road, Even noticed that they were not alone. At first she spotted only a few other travelers, beginning with a woman with a snake's tail instead of legs who carried a patchwork pack over her human shoulder. Slithering over the bricks, she outdistanced them quickly. Even never saw her face. They also passed a tortoise who was twice the size of a car. On his back he was carrying a small island with trees. She thought she saw tiny monkeys swinging from the trees.

Later they saw a herd of horses that looked as if they were made of liquid. As the horses galloped by, they sprayed water into the air and left hoof-size puddles on the bricks.

"Hey, you're supposed to be by the sea!" Jeremy called to them. "Where are you going?"

"Away!" one of them neighed.

Another agreed. "It's not safe anymore!"

They galloped on without answering any more questions.

Continuing, Even, Odd, and Jeremy passed a family of dogs, each with three heads. One puppy barked at them with two of its heads, and its mother shushed it and apologized. "He's anxious," the right head of the mother dog explained. "We've never left home before."

"I know how he feels," Odd said. She held out her hand so the puppy could sniff it. All three heads laid their noses on her palm. One head licked her fingers, and Odd cooed at it as if it were one of her shelter pups. *Guess her knack for animals translates into a knack for magical beings,* Even thought.

The puppy wagged his tail.

"Why are you leaving home?" Even asked the parent dogs.

"We're going to stay with our cousin in New City, at least until things calm down along the border," the mother dog said with her center head. "A pack of werewolves was seen outside our den, and I don't want my pups to have that kind of influence in their life." She lowered her voice so the pups couldn't over-hear. "I also don't want them harmed."

The left head of the father dog growled. "Rotten were-wolves aren't supposed to be hunting in civilized places—that's why there are agreements. Give predators their own areas. But with the border magic still on the fritz, there's no telling where they'll pop up next."

"Yes, I know, but we have to let the Academy of Magic han-dle it," the mother dog said. "They'll send wizards."

"They're overrun with complaints, too tied up in their own bureaucracy," another of the father's heads said. "We should have handled it ourselves, with or without their approval." He snapped the air with his jaws, as if to demonstrate how he'd have handled it.

"That would have been foolish," one of the mother's heads told him.

The two dogs, all mouths talking at once, fell to quarreling. A few of the pups joined in, nipping at one another and occasionally at their own heads. Even raised her voice to wish them luck, but they were too involved to notice.

Jeremy carried Even and Odd until the sun was directly overhead. Rejecting his offer for a cupcake lunch—Jeremy quickly claimed he was joking—they stopped in the next town and bought food with a pouch of coins that Jeremy's mother had given him.

The shop owner was a talking cat. His fur was black-and-white, and his tail had a plaid bow tied to the end of it. It twitched back and forth as if he was nervous. Out of the corner of her eye, Even saw Odd move as if she wanted to pet him but then restrain herself.

"Are you all right?" Odd asked him.

The cat shot glances right and left as if worried he'd be overheard. Also in the shop was a woman with a single eye in the center of her forehead and an older man with tusks protruding between his lips. They were hurriedly pulling together armfuls of loaves of bread and jars of fruit.

"Seen anything?" the cat asked in a hushed voice.

"What kind of anything?" Even asked. Truthfully, they'd seen a lot, but she wasn't sure what the cat was asking. To him, water horses and three-headed dogs were probably normal sights.

"Lots of people coming through scared," the cat said. His fur rippled as he talked, a cat version of a shudder. He glanced again at the tusked man and the cyclops woman. "Frankly, I'm thinking of closing up the store for a few weeks. Until the border magic is working properly again and this all blows over."

"Um, we saw a dragon appear out of nowhere," Jeremy said. "Also, my home switched places with a lake, stranding a school of mermaids and destroying many of our caves."

The cat's tail fluffed even more, burying the plaid bow in fur. "Truly?"

Even wondered if she was always going to recognize emotions in fur. *He's scared*, she thought. *Really scared.* She'd been so focused on getting home that she hadn't thought about how all the turmoil near the border was affecting others. Seeing the worried travelers, and now the shopkeeper, made her want to travel faster. If she and Odd could reach Lady Vell, maybe they could help a lot of people.

"You know I cannot lie, even if I really, really want to," Jeremy said, and then winced. "Not that I want to lie to you. And there really was a dragon. Also, werewolves. A family of three-headed dogs said werewolves had been displaced too and were hunting outside their own territory."

"Dogs! Werewolves!" The shop owner hissed and spat before

composing himself again. "Things are worse than I thought. Take your food and go. I have a family I need to check on." He scampered to the back of his shop.

"Oops," Jeremy said. "Guess I shouldn't have said that."

They waited for a second, half expecting him to return, but when he didn't, they took the food, adding it to Jeremy's satchel on top of his soda and Farmcats cards, and retreated from the shop. "I don't like this," Jeremy said.

"Me neither," Even agreed. "Let's maybe go faster?"

As they continued on, Even watched the numbers of travelers increase. There were plenty of humans, many of whom could have passed for ordinary in the mundane world, as well as a deer with a hundred prongs, a trio of living gargoyles, and a family of horned snakes.

Not travelers, she thought. *Refugees.*

They were fleeing the borderlands, heading for the interior of Firoth, toward the heart of it, where the city lay. She wondered if any of them were also going to see Lady Vell.

She hoped they arrived soon. Surely, if Lady Vell was an expert on border magic, she'd be able to help them as well as everyone they'd passed on the road. Maybe she already knew and was trying to fix the gateways. But if that was happening, why were things worse instead of better?

★★★

As they continued to journey away from the border, the yellow brick road became smoother and better maintained. It gleamed when the sun hit it. In fact, all the colors seemed brighter, and it wasn't just because the sun was rising higher in the sky. *It's the air,* Even thought. It was crisper here, and it made everything feel fresher. The mood of all the travelers on the road seemed lighter too, the farther they journeyed from danger. A few were laughing as their children romped through the fields and meadows. She saw a troll with his child riding on his shoulders, fifteen feet in the air, as well as a group of dryads chattering as they walked along.

"Ugh, I hate the smell," Jeremy complained. "The farther from the border you go, the more sickly sweet it gets."

"It's like everything's soaked in perfume," Odd said.

"I think it smells nice," Even said. Honestly, did they have to criticize everything? "Where's it coming from?"

"Flower fairies," Jeremy said. "Overpopulation of them." He nodded his head toward a field as they trotted past. It was blanketed in flowers, and they looked to be in motion. As Even stared, she realized that not everything that looked like a flower actually was one — a large number of the flowers were actually fairies with bodies made of petals. They flitted from blossom to blossom. With each plant they touched, more blooms appeared, great swaths of yellow then red then purple.

"I think it's beautiful," Even said. She glared at Odd and

Jeremy, daring them to contradict her. Sure, maybe flower fairies bit, but they were still extraordinary.

"Want to do something fun?" Jeremy asked. He didn't wait
for them to answer. He abruptly turned off the road and ran
into the field.

The flower fairies shrieked and rose up into the air. The
mass of them was so thick that it was like a colorful cloud of
pinks and purples and blues and yellows.

"Jeremy, what are you doing?" Odd yelled as she clung to his
back. "We'll get bitten!"

"Not if I'm fast enough! Hang on!" He ran in a circle. The
flower fairies flew with him, circling until they formed a colorful cyclone. Laughing, he burst through the cyclone and ran
back to the road. Within the cyclone, the fairies were laughing
and singing, their voices like high-pitched bells. It sounded like
a thousand wind chimes chiming all at once.

Even twisted to see behind her as the flower-fairy cyclone
dispersed, all the colors mixed. Across the field, it was now a
riot of every color imaginable, as if someone had flung many
colors of paint onto a canvas at once.

"You just need to be quick enough so they don't remember
they have teeth," Jeremy said.

He carried them back to the road.

Odd looked back at the field. "That was . . ."

Even expected her to scold him, say he could have trampled

the fairies, say they needed to stay on the road and not be distracted, or say that the fairies were ridiculous, but instead Odd said, "That was awesome!"

"You think so?" Even said.

"We painted the sky! And look at the field!"

It was the first time in months that Odd had said she liked anything magical, and the second time she'd shown any excitement about something in Firoth. *Five things I'm grateful for,* Even thought. *Number one: I'm here with my sister.*

***

By mid-afternoon, they saw the city, and all Even could think was, *Wow!*

It looked as if New York City had been dipped in glitter. Gold and silver towers shone in the sunlight. A steady stream of magical beings walked, galloped, slithered, scurried, and flew on the yellow brick road into and out of the city.

"Never seen that before," Jeremy said.

Even didn't know if he meant the woman with antlers, the snake with nine heads, or the green-skinned two-foot-tall man who carried a singing briefcase. "Seen what?"

He pointed his horn at what looked to Even like a flying surfboard. "One of those. Must be new." As they came close to another board, Jeremy called out, "Whatcha doing?"

The surfer, a hedgehog-like animal covered in golden scales, was reclining on his board with a book propped up on his soft belly. Lowering his book, he peered at them.

Jeremy adjusted his pace so he was trotting at the same speed as the board. "That thing you're riding. You don't seem to be controlling it. What is it? A new kind of magic carpet?"

Even expected the golden hedgehog to tell them to leave him alone—he'd been immersed in a book—but instead the hedgehog looked delighted to be asked. "This?" the hedgehog said, waving his hand at the board. "This is *new!* This is *amazing!* It's not like a magic carpet. It doesn't require a bit of your own magic. You just tell it your destination, then lean back and enjoy. State-of-the-art stuff."

"Like a car!" Jeremy said.

"Not like a car," Odd said. "You have to drive a car. That's nothing like a car."

"What's a car?" the hedgehog asked.

"A car is cool!" Jeremy said. *"Vroom-vroom!"*

Even cleared her throat.

"Oh, sorry!"

"We're looking for a wizard named Lady Vell," Even said to the hedgehog. "She's supposed to live near New City. Have you heard of her? Do you know where we could find her?"

"Ha!" the hedgehog said. "So you're after one of these beauties yourself! I don't blame you. Everyone wants one. What you need to do is go to Lady Vell's estate and get on the list for a free board. You might get lucky. Got mine yesterday. Watch me zoom!" He spurted ahead, shouting, "Woo-hoo!"

Others cleared out of the way as he zipped past.

"Why did he think we wanted a floating surfboard?" Odd asked. "That was *not* what we asked."

"I want one," Jeremy said.

"He seemed to recognize Lady Vell's name," Even said, "so that's a good thing."

"But he didn't give us directions," Odd pointed out.

"Jeremy's parents said she's north of New City," Even said. "So I vote we keep going through the city." She pointed. The yellow brick road plunged straight into the heart of the city. "I'm sure someone will be able to give us directions."

With Even and Odd holding on tight, Jeremy trotted between the silver shiny towers and plunged into the hustle and bustle of a magical city in the middle of an ordinary afternoon. Even didn't know what to look at: the smooth pillar-like towers, the shops that sold potions and flying shoes and elaborate cakes with dancing decorations, or the wizards and mythical creatures who filled the streets and sidewalks. She craned her neck, trying to see everything at once.

Jeremy hailed a man with curled horns and goat legs who seemed to be waving traffic through with extra-hairy arms. "Sir? We're visitors here, and we could use some help."

"Happy to be of service!" the goat-man said. His voice was as high-pitched as a flute, and he sang each word. "What can I do for you?"

"We're looking for someone," Even said, "an expert in border magic. Her name is Lady Vell, but all we know is that we're supposed to go north."

"Ah, yes, of course! Lady Vell!"

"You know her?" Odd asked.

That's lucky, Even thought. It was a big city and seemed stuffed with people and creatures, and so far two of them had recognized Lady Vell's name. She seemed to be more well-known than Even had guessed. No wonder she wasn't answering calls on her mirror.

"I'm thinking of getting one of those boards for myself!" the goat-man said. "They're said to fly themselves, with no magic cost. Height of convenience. And of course my kids all want to play on one. Have you seen them?"

"We've seen them," Even said, "but what exactly do they have to do with Lady Vell?"

"Everything!" the goat-man said. "Just head due north, and you'll find her estate. Got a silver tower and lots of fancy gardens. She's one of those business-entrepreneur wizards, always inventing new stuff. Anyway, you can't miss it. She's been giving away a bunch of boards each day for free, as an advertisement for her newest line of products. There's been a queue outside her front door since sunrise. Everyone in New City wants one of her new free-magic contraptions."

They thanked him, even though at least half of what he'd said made no sense at all. Business-entrepreneur wizard? Free-magic contraption? *This* was the person who was supposed to help send them back across the border, restore the unicorns' and mermaids' homes, and make everything normal again?

12

AS THEY TRAVELED through the city, Even saw more of the flying boards. A dog with tentacles zipped past them on one and performed a loop before riding up the side of a building. An elderly woman rode by on her board at a more leisurely pace. Instead of hair, she had snakes that writhed around her head and hissed at all the pedestrians.

"Those things are everywhere," Jeremy said.

For an instant, Even thought he meant the snake hair, but then she realized he meant the flying boards. She sidestepped a centaur who was selling basketball-size oranges, while a flock of winged horses swooped overhead. Marveling at them, Even asked, "Is New City always like this?"

"You mean crowded?"

"I mean incredible."

"Guess so," Jeremy said. "My parents send me on errands

sometimes. They think it keeps me from daydreaming about living far away." He snorted, as if to say how pointless their efforts were.

Gawking at a half elephant, half tiger, Even tried to imagine what it would have been like to grow up surrounded by this much magic. If her parents hadn't moved to the most boring town in Connecticut, what would her life have been like? Working in the border shop, she'd seen a lot of magical beings, but this . . . Everywhere she turned, she saw another creature who looked as if he or she had walked, flown, or slithered straight out of her dreams. "I don't get why you don't see how amazing this place is."

"Eh, it's home. How can I be impressed with home?"

Even waved her hand at all of it. "You aren't impressed with *this*?"

"Are *you* impressed with your cars and traffic lights and dumpsters? Not to mention soda and Farmcats cards? You don't see how amazing *your* world is."

Odd spoke up. "I do. Even, you still want to go home, right? You're worrying me."

Glancing at her, Even saw she had water pooling in her eyes. "Of course I want to go home!" She wanted that just as badly as Odd did. Odd had to know that.

Or maybe she didn't know that. After all, it wasn't a secret that Even had wanted to come back to Firoth and see the world she could barely remember. *And it is as wondrous as I dreamed,* she thought.

Beside them, a giant otter scampered along the sidewalk. Miniscule griffins darted from window ledge to window ledge. Trees with flowers that resembled bells lined the street. Vendors were hawking pastries that looked like castles, fruit that shone like jewels, and breads that baked on their plates, rising and browning without an oven. Beneath their carts, pixies —pigeon-size, all-blue fairies with sharp teeth—scavenged for stray crumbs and squabbled over their finds.

But, as wondrous as it was, Even still wanted to find Lady Vell and go home. Of course she did. Didn't she? She thought of Mom and Dad. She missed them. And her home—she missed her room, her bed. She even missed their bathroom. And of course she missed their shop. She loved that place with its stuffed shelves and weird mix of magic and mundane.

A phoenix—a bird with feathers of fire—flew like a comet above the city. Even watched it blaze across the blue-green sky.

No, she thought, correcting herself. *I don't just want to go home. I want the border to be open and stay open so I can come back.*

I want both.

"Do we join the line?" Jeremy asked.

Ahead of them, north of the city, was a tree-edged road. A queue of Firothans—humans, fairies, centaurs, fauns, oversize spiders, and countless others—snaked down it toward a grand estate. At the end of the driveway, a lone silver tower, twisted like a spiral shell, sat amid beautiful gardens and manicured trees.

"That must be Lady Vell's estate," Jeremy guessed. "Let's find whoever is in charge and tell them we want to talk to Lady Vell."

"We can say the unicorns sent us," Even said.

"It is true," Jeremy said.

It had been Even's idea to come, but Starry had approved it and Effervescent Spring had suggested Jeremy take them. "If the goat-man's right, all these people are here for her boards," Even said. "So we can skip the line since we're not interested in them."

"Well, I'm kind of interested," Jeremy said.

Even and Odd dismounted and then, together with Jeremy, walked the length of the line. At the front, blocking the wide-as-a-horse door to the tower, was a centaur. Sweaty, with his hair sticking to his cheeks and his tail swatting at his rump, he was trying to talk to multiple people at once. "I'll add you to the list," he said to one; "You can't jump ahead," to another; "I can't make it happen faster, but I'll add you to the list," to a third.

"Excuse me?" Even called, trying to catch the centaur's attention.

"Hey! You can't cut!" the woman who was next in line yelled.

"Please, we just want to go home," Odd pleaded.

"We're here to talk to Lady Vell," Even said loudly. "On behalf of the unicorns who live near the border. And ourselves."

"I'll add you to the list," the centaur said, tired.

"You can't just let them cut!" the woman said. "I've been waiting for hours!"

Even pleaded with the centaur. "The border gateways are closed, and we're on the wrong side! We're trying to get home, and we can't. We were told Lady Vell might be able to help us. Please, can you ask Lady Vell if she'll see us?"

"All I can do is add you to the list. Names?"

"Even and Odd Berry. And this is Jeremy from Unicorn Hill."

"Even and Odd? Berry?" the centaur repeated. He squinted at them as if finally seeing them, but Even couldn't tell what he was thinking. She was glad she wasn't still a skunk. "Any relation to Janet and Sunny Berry?"

"They're our parents!" Odd said. "Do you know them?"

"Not personally," the centaur said as he made a note. "You're on the list."

The woman pushed forward. "Not fair! I'm next!" She threw open her cape, and an octopus-like tentacle shot out, aiming to grab the centaur's list. He reared back, and she missed, instead knocking it out of his hands.

Concentrating, Even tried to catch the list with her mind, to float it back to the centaur, but she wasn't the only one with magic. The list flew through the air and landed in the hands of a man a dozen people back. He returned it to the centaur.

"You will *not* be added to today's list," the centaur told the tentacle woman. "Please do not return until you can act more civilized."

Grumbling, the tentacle woman retreated.

"Please, can't you help us?" Even asked the centaur.

"We just want to go home," Odd said.

The centaur sighed. "Lady Vell is an important woman with many demands on her time. She distributes gifts through me. She does not receive visitors." He raised his voice and boomed, using magic to make his words project across the manicured gardens all the way down the tree-lined driveway, "I will present the list to Lady Vell! Those who are chosen will receive boards. The rest of you who did not make today's list, go home and return tomorrow."

"We *can't* go home!" Even said. "That's why we have to talk to her now!"

But the centaur clopped into the silver tower and shut the thick silver door behind him. Grumbling, the crowd began to disperse. Those who had made the list lingered in hopes of being chosen, while the rest trudged back toward the city.

"Well, that failed," Jeremy said.

"It can't fail," Odd cried. "It was our only idea!"

They stared up at the spiral tower. There were no windows,

and the smooth twisted silver reminded Even of a spaceship. It looked impenetrable, even by the atmosphere. She didn't know if Lady Vell was inside, if she knew there were people who needed her help, if she cared at all.

At least the centaur put us on the list, she thought. Would he tell Lady Vell they were here for help, not for one of her boards? Would it matter? "We'll give the centaur a chance to talk to her, and then we'll try again." They'd try as many times as it took.

They waited for the centaur to reappear.

And waited.

Some of the magical beings who'd wanted free boards drifted back to the city, but others stayed, hopeful, as Even, Odd, and Jeremy were, that the centaur would open the door again. A few creatures zoomed around on their already-claimed boards, over topiaries and rosebushes, while a six-foot-tall rabbit in a tie adjusted a mirror as if it were a camera recording their tricks. Others milled around in front of the silver tower, in a loose sort of line.

A blue-skinned man with multiple eyes on his forehead shoved a loaf of bread at Even. "Trade for bread?" He was pulling a cart piled with baked goods.

"No thanks."

"Blackbird bread," he said, waving it.

"Not interested."

The bread split, and a bird poked its head through the crust, beak-first. It chirped at Even as it shook off the crust and flew toward the sky, disappearing into the clouds. Several hungry pixies chased after it.

"Very no thanks," Odd said.

The man blinked with all his eyes at once, shrugged, and said, "Suit yourself. But wait here long enough, and you'll change your mind." Leaving them, he approached the rabbit with the mirror, who also shooed him away.

"I'm not waiting long enough to eat *that*," Odd said. Marching up to the door, she knocked on it. Even joined her, knocking as well. The door clanged like it was made of metal, like they were thumping on the hood of a car.

"Lady Vell!" Even called as they knocked. "Please, we need your help!"

"It's an emergency!" Odd called.

No one answered.

They stepped back. Even rubbed the side of her fist. She'd been knocking so hard that it ached. Maybe the centaur wasn't going to open the door again. Maybe Lady Vell wasn't going to agree to see them. Maybe Jeremy's parents had been right, and they should have stayed at Unicorn Hill and waited for the grownups to figure out how to help them.

The door slid open a crack, and the centaur poked his head out. "You said you're the Berry children?" he asked.

"Yes, that's us!" Even said. She wondered why he'd recognized their name. It had been surprising enough that Jeremy's mom knew about them. Just how well known was the story of their split magic? And when had Mom and Dad planned to tell them the truth?

"Please, we need to speak with Lady Vell!" Odd said.

"And she would like to speak with you." Checking to make sure no one else was near, the centaur slid open the door wider. "Please, come inside."

13

'LOCKS SNAPPED INTO place up the sides and around
the top of the enormous door, and Even felt a wiggle of nervousness. She knew the locks were to keep the eager public out,
but she couldn't help noticing that they also kept her, Odd, and
Jeremy in. "Lady Vell doesn't like visitors?" she asked.

"She prefers her admirers to keep their distracting noise
outside," the centaur said. "I am, in fact, the only one she typically allows within her sanctuary. Her genius requires intense
concentration."

"My genius requires fresh clover," Jeremy offered.

Odd shushed him.

The centaur led them through a darkened hallway, pushed
open another door, and held it for them. Even went first and
halted, blinking in the light, as the hallway opened into a vast
room with a ceiling hundreds of feet high.

She took a few more steps inside and ducked as a pink bird swooped over her head. In its wake, the bird left a contrail of sparkling blue that lingered in the air like floating glitter.

The vast space was filled with rows of laboratory tables. Half of them were filled with bottles and tubes and jars; the rest were piled high with wires, wheels, and scraps of metal. It looked like a cross between a garage, a chemist's lab, and a modern-art gallery.

In the center of the lab was a twelve-foot-tall glass vat. It was filled with a bubbling liquid the same color as the bright blue that sparkled in the air.

"Is it me, or does this all give off a strong 'mad scientist' vibe?" Odd murmured behind her.

"It's not you," Even whispered back.

Clip-clopping across the laboratory, the centaur said, "I will inform Lady Vell of your arrival. Touch nothing." He disappeared through a doorway that Even hadn't noticed, on the opposite side of the lab.

Coming farther in, she approached the vat of bubbling blue. Several of the flying boards were soaking in it. A stack of others lay on a nearby worktable.

"Whoa, cool," Jeremy said, trotting up to stare at the boards. "How fast do you think they go? And how do you steer them?"

"Hey, Even, look at this," Odd said.

Even crossed to Odd. She was bending over a worktable that held what looked like a three-dimensional map. Even recognized it from her Academy textbooks. "It's Firoth."

She heard a clatter behind her, and the two girls spun around to see Jeremy standing in the aftermath of an avalanche of flying boards. "Oops," he said.

He began to push the boards back into a stack, using his horn and hooves.

"Try to be more careful," Odd told him.

"Sorry."

Even and Odd helped him neaten the pile before returning to the map.

"I think we're here," Even said, pointing to where she thought the capital city was. She traced the road they'd taken to New City back to where they'd entered Firoth. The border was marked in red. Towns were labeled in black. She wondered if every town close to the border had its own gateway. "Can we use this to find the other gateways?" she wondered.

"What would it matter, if they're all closed?" Odd asked.

"If Lady Vell can help, then it will matter." Even reached out to touch the lake in the map and was startled when it felt wet on her fingertip. She stared at it more intently. It almost looked as if . . . "I can see the mermaids!"

"Really?" Leaning closer, Odd bumped her head against

Even's. They both squinted at the tiny shapes that swam through the miniature lake.

Behind them, they heard another clatter and then Jeremy: "Sorry, sorry."

Glancing over her shoulder, Even saw the boards were spilled across the floor again.

"I'll clean it up," Jeremy promised. "Don't worry about me."

Even and Odd turned back to studying the map.

"Do you think we're looking at the real lake?" Odd asked.

"Can't be," Even said, reading the label on the town next to it. "The real lake isn't in Lakeview anymore."

"Oh, right. So it's an inaccurate magic map."

It was Firoth as it was supposed to be, with no displaced mermaids or unicorns or goblins or dragons. *It's beautiful,* Even thought. "Goal is to make it accurate again. If the border reopens, do you think all the displaced land and creatures will shift back to where they're supposed to be?"

"No idea," Odd said.

"Maybe Lady Vell will know."

At the next table, they saw a stack of dishes and a bucket of blue soapy water. The dishes were dipping themselves into the bucket so hard that they cracked. A towel dried the shattered dishes, and the shards stacked themselves. Beyond that was a table with a pile of dolls. As they walked up to it, one of the dolls waddled across the table toward them. Odd shrieked and jumped back.

"I wuv you!" it cried in a squeaky voice.

Arms out, it hugged the air as it toppled off the edge of the table. It landed with a soft *whoomp*, and the other dolls chorused, "I wuv you!"

"That could not be more creepy," Odd noted.

Finished restacking the boards, Jeremy rejoined them. He shooed one of the dolls away by flicking his tail. "Don't you have things like that in the mundane world? Toys that move and talk?"

"Not exactly the same," Odd said, and shuddered.

Even spotted a dribble of bright blue on one of the dolls' mouths. "I think it's all connected to that." She pointed to the blue vat.

"What is that stuff?" Odd asked.

Both of them looked at Jeremy. He tossed his mane, the equivalent to a shrug. "Never seen it before. Kind of looks like soda. Except not a flavor I'd want to drink." Losing interest in the blue bubbles, he began examining the various contraptions on the tables.

Circling the vat, Even saw a tube piping the bubbling blue into it. She followed it toward its source, across the room to a pedestal that held a heart-size black stone, which sparked as if it were electrified.

"Looks like the blue stuff is coming from over here," Even called. "Not sure how a stone makes fizzy blue soda, though. Weird." She felt like she'd seen the black stone before. She couldn't explain it, but there was something so familiar about it. She had a strange feeling that the stone belonged to her, even though she was positive she'd never owned a magically sparking rock.

Odd joined her. "Looks like it's surrounded by . . . well, it kind of looks like a force field. Do magical force fields exist?"

"I don't know," Even said. "That's way beyond level-five magic."

The air around the pedestal shimmered, as if the stone were encased in a giant bubble, blocking her from coming any closer than five feet. Tentatively, she reached out a finger, wondering if it would pop—

A voice said behind them, "Fascinating."

Jumping, both Even and Odd spun around to face an elegant woman in a silk robe with fur at its cuffs. She wore a necklace of fist-size bubbles, each with a drop of bright blue suspended in the center. Diamonds dotted her cheeks, as if glued to her skin, and her hair was pinned back with an assortment of tools: screwdrivers, wrenches, tiny hammers.

"I had wondered if you two little darlings would be drawn to the power stone someday, by curiosity if nothing else," the woman said, "and here you are. Do you remember it? You were very young, so it wouldn't be surprising if you don't."

"Lady Vell?" Even guessed.

"But of course. And you must be, as you're so charmingly known, Even and Odd." She smiled at them as if they were the most delightful sight she'd seen all day. "Which is which? And is it an even day or an odd day? I assume it does not follow the calendar?"

"Even, and it's my day," Even said. As proof, she concentrated on one of the nearby dolls. Rising into the air, it waved its cloth hand and repeated, "I wuv you."

Lady Vell clasped her hands to her heart. "Adorable! I do not understand why children haven't warmed to them. You think they're precious, don't you?"

The sisters exchanged glances.

"Sure," Odd said.

"They'd give me nightmares," Jeremy volunteered.

Both Even and Odd glared at him.

Lady Vell pretended he hadn't spoken. "They come already powered. The owner simply has to bring it back for recharging every few weeks. It is perfect for the child who lacks their own magic." She swept her arms out wide to encompass the whole of her workshop. "That is the aim of much of what you see here: pre-powered conveniences and delights, to be enjoyed either by those who cannot afford to expend the extra magic or by those who have no magic to begin with." She frowned as a dish shattered in the nearby bucket and the pieces stacked themselves neatly on a pile of broken plates. "Of course, some refinements are needed, but such is the price of progress. You've seen my transportation devices?"

"The floating surfboards?" Even asked.

"Transportation devices," Lady Vell corrected. "Yes. Those have been my most popular offering, but there's more to come! And you, my dears, will be part of it all! At least in your own small way."

"Sorry?" Odd said.

"Come, relax in my solarium. We'll get to know one another." Glancing at the boards that had been restacked (badly) twice, she said with a hint of distaste, "Bring your unicorn friend, if you wish." She swept them across the vast workroom and through the doorway that the centaur had used. It led to a small room next to the laboratory.

Inside, the solarium glowed with a warm amber light. Potted trees swayed side to side as if to unheard music. Butterflies made of paper flitted from flower to flower, and more of the sparkling birds flew overhead. Flowering vines hung from the ceiling, and a few of the flowers were singing a wordless tune. Everything, Even noticed, glinted with a bit of sparkling blue.

"Lady Vell, we were told you're an expert in border magic," Even said. "And we're hoping you can help all the people and creatures in the borderlands, including a lake full of mermaids, a hill full of unicorns, and others."

"And us!" Odd said. "We need to get home. We're not supposed to be here."

"On the contrary, this is your birth land," Lady Vell said. "You are very welcome here."

"Our home is in a town in Connecticut," Even said. "Our parents run a shop there, across the border." And that border was supposed to be open.

"Ah!" Lady Vell looked as pleased as a cat with milk, which Even thought was a strange reaction. Why did she care about their store? "I had heard your lovely parents' shop was thriving. I am so happy that their life change was a success."

"You know our parents?" Odd said. "Do you know where our mom is?"

"She needs to be able to go home too," Even said. "But according to the unicorns, the gateways are closed everywhere."

"You were so young when you moved," Lady Vell said. "But you'll find that this world will welcome you. You belong here, and I know you'll be happy." She smiled at them, spread her silk robe, and sat in one of the chairs. "And I am in a position to ensure that your lives here are comfortable." Clapping her hands to summon the centaur, Lady Vell smiled at both sisters.

The centaur bustled forward with a tray of glasses and tiny sandwiches. For Jeremy, he brought a bucket of fresh clover. The unicorn immediately stuck his face in the bucket and began chomping. Belatedly, he said, "Thanks. Long journey."

"Sit. Eat," Lady Vell said to the girls. "Relax."

"I'm sorry, but we can't stay," Even said. "Please, do you know how to fix the gateways? There are people who need to get across the border." She told Lady Vell about the elf priestess and Mr. Fratelli's daughter, as well as the centaurs with their research. "It's not just us. Lots of people need your help."

Lady Vell nibbled on a sandwich. "Mmm, delicious."

Even and Odd exchanged glances. Both of them sat in the plush chairs opposite the tray. Trying to be polite, Even helped herself to a sandwich layered with pasta and some kind of meatballs. She bit into it, and she tasted a burst of blueberries, honey, and cheese. "Delicious," she said. "Thank you."

Smiling graciously at her, Lady Vell said, "I am, as you may have guessed from my home, a wealthy woman. I can ensure that you and your mother have everything you need for a life of comfort anywhere in the magic world you want. You like the bustle of the capital? I can buy you a home in the heart of the markets so there is always a festival outside your door. You want natural beauty and serenity? How about your own island, full of birds that sing you to sleep and a sea full of wonders? Or do you prefer the mountains—"

"We don't want to stay," Odd said.

Lady Vell frowned, puckering her lips. A tiny jewel popped off her cheek. "I don't think you understand. I am offering you luxury. All I need is one teensy-tiny favor in return."

"What kind of favor?" Even asked. Odd shot her a look, but Even ignored it. *I'm not going to say yes,* she wished she could say out loud to Odd. She wasn't going to agree to anything that stood in the way of them getting home. Odd should know her well enough to realize that. *I just want to know what she wants.*

"An easy one that won't cost you anything but a minute of your time," Lady Vell said, beaming at them both. "All I want is a statement. One itsy-bitsy public statement in front of a magic mirror so that the voting members of the Academy of Magic will see. All I want is for you to simply introduce yourselves and state that you have suffered no ill effects from the accident that occurred in your youth."

"We don't remember that," Even said.

"Ah, but you have lived with the results." Lady Vell squeezed her sandwich so hard in her excitement that the innards squirted through her fingers. A dollop of jam landed on her foot, sliding between the jewels on her sandals. She appeared not to notice. "You share your magic on alternating days. There have been no side effects other than that, have there?"

"No other side effects," Even said, and Odd nodded too.

"And those days you have magic, does it feel like it's yours?"

"Yes, of course," Even said. *It is mine,* she thought. *It should have been all mine.* But she pushed that thought aside to deal with later.

Beaming at them, Lady Vell clapped her hands. "Wonderful!"

"I don't understand," Even said. "Why would anyone care about whether we've had side effects from something that happened so long ago we don't remember it?"

Instead of answering, Lady Vell asked, "Did you not recognize the power stone, the one you were examining just now?"

"You mean the stone with the lightning?" Even asked. She *had* felt as if there was something familiar about the stone, but she had no idea why. "Should we have?"

"Power stones are rare—your parents used this very same one in their experiments. It was that stone that caused your powers to be split and shared. Your parents tried everything they could think of to reverse the effects of what they'd done, but eventually they despaired. With the goal of giving you a fresh start, they decided to leave the magic world and open a border store in the mundane world, abandoning all their research and all they could have accomplished. I bought the power stone from them. They intended to use the profit to set up new lives for all of you."

"We have those lives," Odd said. "We *like* those lives."

Mostly, Even amended silently.

As if Odd hadn't spoken, Lady Vell continued. "Unfortunately, after the accident, the Academy forbade anyone from ever repeating their work. It was thought the cost was too high —that's nonsense, of course. But the narrow-minded fools at the

Academy have always been risk-averse to the point of stifling progress. It was only with tremendous and tireless effort that I was able to obtain a temporary license for experimentation. So if you could simply speak publicly about your experience, that would prove to the Academy of Magic that my experiments on the power stone are perfectly safe. My temporary license would be upgraded to permanent, and I would be able to proceed with my research with the full support of the Academy."

"What exactly does a power stone do?" Even asked.

"It redistributes magic," Lady Vell said. "Used correctly, a power stone will siphon magic from one source and make it available for use in another way. I have been employing it to extract power from a previously untapped resource, collect it here"—she waved her hand toward her laboratory—"and fuel a myriad of wonderful, new inventions that will revolutionize the world!"

That all sounded good, but . . . what untapped resource? Lady Vell, the unicorns had said, was an expert on border magic. An uncomfortable idea was taking shape in Even's mind. "Did you . . . Is it your fault the border is closed?" Even winced as the words came out of her mouth. She didn't know how to make her guess sound less accusatory.

Jeremy's head shot up from the bucket of clover. "What?"

Lady Vell sipped from her tea. "Indirectly, yes," she said, calmly.

"You caused this!" Odd jumped up, knocking several sandwiches from the tray.

"The closing of the border is an unfortunate side effect, which I acknowledge has caused some inconveniences," Lady Vell said.

"My home *moved!*" Jeremy said. He pranced in place, agitated, clover forgotten. "Unicorn Hill switched places with a lake. That's more than an *inconvenience!* Many of our caves collapsed, and others are about to!"

"And the mermaids in the lake can't get to fresh food," Even added. "A dragon popped up out of nowhere — and it was *angry!* The road from the border is filled with refugees who lost their homes or are fleeing danger."

Putting her teacup down, Lady Vell waved her hand in the air dismissively. "Everyone will get used to their new homes and adjust to the changes."

"But . . . you're destroying homes! And separating families!" Odd said. "On purpose!"

"You children are not understanding the importance of what I'm doing here. Come with me. I feel the need to point dramatically at the source of my success." Lady Vell led the way back to the sparking stone. She halted outside the glimmering bubble that surrounded it. "For the past eight years, I have been studying the power stone, dreaming of the possibilities if one could harness its power to transfer magic. After rigorous experimentation, I have adapted it in a new way: I am mining the border magic." She pointed to the tube that led to the vat of bubbling blue. "By immersing items in border magic, I can imbue them with their own power. It's an untapped resource that has the capacity to change the lives of the magicless and to improve the lives of everyone!"

"You're stealing border magic," Even said, "and that's why the gateways closed. You're siphoning the magic away. You caused the chaos! It's all your fault!"

Lady Vell frowned, and wrinkles sprouted between her eyebrows. "I thought you'd be pleased that the stone that failed you in your youth is now being used for good."

"This is *not* good!" Odd said. "It's keeping us prisoner here!"

Lady Vell laughed. "Children are so melodramatic. You are hardly prisoners. You're in a world of magic and wonder. So much to explore and enjoy! You should be thanking me."

"You're hurting people," Even said.

"And unicorns," Jeremy put in.

"Pish-posh, nonsense," Lady Vell said. "I thought you would *want* to help further the research into the magic that helped shape your lives. But all I hear are complaints."

"We can't go home—" Odd began.

"Contact your mother, enjoy your life here, and try to be more grateful." Lady Vell signaled to the centaur. "I will win the Academy's approval without your assistance. It would have made things easier to have your testimony, but you aren't essential. The people love my creations, and that should suffice. Popular opinion has power, you know, and thanks to my daily giveaways, my boards have many fans."

"Lady Vell, please," Even begged, "you can't take magic from the border! The gateways need to be open! The unicorns said the problems caused by the lack of border magic will spread, and you know they can't lie."

"Conjecture based on no evidence," Lady Vell said dismissively. "Yes, mining the border magic has caused side effects, but we are only talking about a small number of inconsequential beings. There's no proof the instability will widen."

Jeremy reared onto his hind legs and then landed with a *thump*. "My family is not inconsequential!"

"To you, perhaps," Lady Vell said. "But to society as a whole? For there to be progress, the few must make sacrifices for the convenience of the many. You will understand when you're older. Choices must be made."

"You're making the wrong one," Odd said.

"Yeah," Even said. "You don't know that the damage won't spread. You're just hoping! You have no idea how bad the effects could be. You're just doing what you want without caring about anyone else. The border magic isn't yours to take!"

Lady Vell clucked her tongue. "The border magic belongs to no one; therefore, there is no law saying I cannot claim it. I do not like the tone you are taking. I invited you as my guests, and now I must ask you to leave." She signaled to the centaur.

He trotted toward them. "This way, please."

Odd's hands were in fists at her sides, and her cheeks were streaked with angry tears. "I want to go home. Please let me go home!"

"Can't you see what you're doing is wrong?" Even cried. "You're stealing the border magic, and it's doing terrible things to people's families and homes. Our family and home! And Jeremy's! And countless others! You have to stop! You can't just turn your back on all of us!"

But Lady Vell did exactly that. Her back to them, she walked away with her silk robe billowing behind her, while the centaur herded the sisters toward the entrance.

We have to stop this! What she's doing is wrong! Concentrating, Even focused on the power stone. If she could transform it into something else . . . She pictured a ketchup bottle.

Stopping, Lady Vell snapped, "Quit your foolish efforts. Not even the strongest magic can touch the stone. It's behind my own protective shield. I don't take chances with something that will revolutionize the world." She flicked her wrist, and the three of them were whooshed backwards out of the workroom and down the hall. The door opened, and they flew outside.

The door slammed shut.

Even, Odd, and Jeremy stared up at the silver tower.

"She caused it," Jeremy said, shock in his voice.

"And she has no intention of fixing it," Even said, feeling sick. She reached over and took Odd's hand. Odd squeezed her hand back. But it didn't make Even feel better.

14

"SHE DOESN'T CARE about who she's hurting," Even said, as they stared up at the tower. How could you just . . . not care? "We have to tell people what she's doing. If they know she's responsible for the border closing, they'll stop her."

Odd shouted, "Hey, everyone!"

A few of the creatures around the tower turned their heads. Most didn't pay any attention. They were treating Lady Vell's estate like a public park, picnicking and partying while they waited for more boards to be distributed. *Bribes,* Even realized. *The boards are bribes.* Lady Vell had talked about popular opinion. *She's giving them away so people will ignore the harm she's doing.*

"Lady Vell is stealing border magic!" Odd shouted.

"She caused the gateways to close!" Even joined in. "She's the reason people can't get home to their families. And she's the reason the borderlands are becoming unstable!"

She saw a few bystanders whisper to one another, but most simply went back to whatever they had been doing: chatting, snacking, playing, waiting. "They don't realize we're serious."

"They're telling the truth!" Jeremy shouted, but no one was paying attention anymore.

"This isn't going to work," Odd said. "We need lots of people to listen and to know we're serious. Everyone can see how fun the boards are, but they don't know the cost. Jeremy, you're from here. How can we get people to listen?"

"Uh, I don't know."

Chewing on her lower lip, Even considered it. "Lady Vell wanted us to give a statement on her behalf in front of a magic mirror saying that what she's doing is safe, so that the Academy of Magic would see and approve of her actions. So what if we do the opposite and find a magic mirror and tell the Academy that she's misusing magic?"

Surely, the Academy of Magic would listen. Even had heard and read so many stories about their wizards: taming out-of-control hydras, stopping a gorgon who kept turning beings into stone, relocating entire elven villages in danger of magic-caused flooding. In every story, the Academy always sent wizards who swooped in to save the day. *If we can tell them what's happening here, they'll appoint a hero to stop Lady Vell from draining the border.*

"Love it," Odd said. "So where do we find a mirror?"

"Back home," Jeremy said. "At Unicorn Hill."

"I mean here. Now."

Even scanned the gardens. Hadn't she seen . . . ? "There. He has a mirror."

She pointed at the six-foot-tall rabbit in his tie. He was still aiming his mirror at kids doing tricks on their floating boards. Two of the kids looked human. One had tentacles instead of arms, and a fourth kid was half goat. The goat-boy rode his board vertically up a lamppost, posed at the top, and dismounted with a somersault. The others whistled and clapped, and a girl zipped her board up the trunk of a tree as if she were in a snowboard halfpipe.

"Ooh, even better, he's a reporter," Jeremy said. "See his badge?"

"That's perfect," Even said. A reporter could tell everyone at once, including the Academy. "Come on!" She motioned for the others to follow her. She marched across the grass. "Excuse me!" She waved, trying to catch the rabbit's attention. "Hi! Mr. Reporter? We have news."

"Yeah, yeah, kid, so does everybody," the rabbit said, eyes on the boarders. "Get out of my shot." He shouldered past them and repositioned his mirror. The boy with tentacles was riding his board upside down. He clung to it with his tentacles.

"Lady Vell is separating families," Even said loudly. "And causing people to lose their homes. Destabilizing the land. How's that for news?"

The rabbit paused. "Okay, I'm intrigued. Sounds like a pretty good story. If it's true."

"It's true," Jeremy confirmed.

"We just spoke with her," Odd said, "and she confessed everything. She doesn't care about the consequences of her actions. She just cares about her 'inventions.'"

The rabbit studied Jeremy. "People will believe it if it comes from the unicorn," he said. The rabbit thumped his hind paw, obviously excited. "Yeah, that's an excellent idea. If the unicorn is your spokesman, then I'll do it."

Unicorns can't lie, Even thought. Of course! It was perfect. Jeremy could explain everything, as well as repeat what Lady Vell had said. "Jeremy, let him interview you! You can tell them what's happening at the border, what happened to us, and what happened your home." He knew about Mr. Fratelli and the lightless fairies. He'd met both Frank and the elf priestess. Plus he'd witnessed the effects of the lake and hill relocating. He could also talk about their encounter with the dragon. If that didn't impress viewers, she didn't know what would.

Talking to himself, the rabbit began to set up the mirror. "Ooh, this is going to be good. Exactly the twist my broadcasts need. This will catch people's attention!"

Jeremy began to tremble from his mane to his tail. "Uh, slight problem."

Odd patted his neck. "Hey, calm down. What's wrong?"

"Mirror shy?" the rabbit asked. "Buck up, kid. This is your chance to be famous. My news reports beam to every mirror in every house, business, and hovel. You'll be seen by thousands! Your folks back home will be amazed."

His eyes wide, Jeremy asked softly, "Even, Odd, can I talk to you a second?"

"Uh, sure," Even said.

They retreated from the reporter.

"What's wrong?" Odd asked.

"I can't do this," Jeremy said.

"Why not?" Even asked. The reporter was offering them the perfect opportunity! It was exactly what they needed to do to reach the people who could fix this mess.

"Because I always crack under pressure," he squeaked. "You've seen me. I babble when I'm stressed and say the wrong thing at the wrong time. What if I say the wrong thing now? What if I mess it all up? What if people don't listen to me? Or what if they *do* and those people are my parents, and they find out I was in your world? What if they're angry with me? What if Lady Vell is? What if everyone is? What if I make things worse?"

He's scared, Even realized. The rabbit was right. Mirror shy. She opened her mouth to say he had to do it anyway, that this was important, but Odd was already talking.

"You can do this," Odd said. "I know you can! All you have to do is describe what you've seen. Just tell people the truth." She was using her encouraging-a-stray-puppy voice.

"But . . . but this is important!" Jeremy said. "And all I'm good at is putting my hoof in my mouth and messing up!"

Odd positioned herself directly in front of him. "Jeremy, remember when you talked about wanting to be in our world so that you could be different and better? The thing is, being there —being different—wouldn't make you better. You keep saying you aren't good under pressure, but look at everything you've done already: coming to our world alone, helping us reach your parents and then the city, escaping the dragon. Remember that? You saved us. Here and now you have a chance to save everyone. And who could do better than that?"

Jeremy was drinking in her words, but he was still trembling.

It's working, Even thought. *Keep talking, Odd.*

Odd laid her hand on his mane. "We'll help you. We'll ask you questions, and you answer. Just talk to us. You don't even have to look at the reporter or the mirror. Keep your eyes on me."

Quietly, the reporter positioned the mirror beside them, just out of Jeremy's line of sight. *Good,* Even thought. So far, Jeremy hadn't noticed him. "How about we practice?" She glanced at the reporter, pointed to the mirror, and mouthed, *Do it!*

"Let's begin at the beginning," Odd said, keeping her eyes on Jeremy and only on him so that he looked back only at her. "How did you meet us?"

"I . . . I came to your border shop."

"And why did you come?"

"At first, I went to your shop because I wanted to buy Farm-cats cards and soda," Jeremy said. "But then I couldn't get back. I thought your father could help."

Odd continued. "Who was in the border shop with you?"

"A centaur and an elf."

"And why were they there?"

With Odd coaching him, Jeremy described everything he'd seen: the centaur who couldn't use his glamour spell, the fairies whose lights were out, the gateway that flickered open and then closed, the lake and the hill that had switched places, the hungry mermaids, the angry displaced dragon, the scared travelers . . . all of it.

And the reporter broadcast every bit of it to mirrors across Firoth.

As Jeremy talked, a small crowd began to gather, mostly kids and teens, some human and many not. They listened. By now Even thought that Jeremy must have guessed that this wasn't practice, but he kept his eyes on Odd as she stroked his mane and nodded, and he kept going, without babbling, without panicking.

"And then when we got back to the city, we started seeing these flying boards . . ."

Even wondered who was seeing the broadcast. How quickly could the Academy of Magic send someone to stop Lady Vell?

"What brought you here, outside Lady Vell's tower?" Odd asked. "You said you traveled to the city with us. Why?"

"My parents said she's a known expert on border magic," Jeremy said. "They couldn't reach her by mirror, so we wanted to try in person. We thought she'd be able to help."

"And what did she say when we asked for help?" Even asked.

"She told us that she is using a power stone to siphon magic from the border. That's how she's creating the floating boards that everyone loves so much, as well as a whole bunch of new inventions she plans to sell."

The little crowd gasped.

Jeremy was beginning to fidget, shifting from hoof to hoof. Even imagined it was getting harder to pretend he was just talking to Odd. She glanced at the door to Lady Vell's tower. It hadn't reopened, and she didn't see the centaur butler. Did Lady Vell know what they were doing? Was she watching from within her tower?

"And what's the problem with that?" Odd prompted.

"The border magic is what keeps the gateways open," Jeremy said. "Without it, people can't travel between worlds. Worse, the magic can't travel between worlds. That means no magic in the mundane world. And it means the borderlands have become unstable, without their connection to the mundane world. People's homes have been moving around, and creatures —sometimes dangerous creatures—are popping up where they don't belong. And it's her fault, and she doesn't care! She has to stop stealing border magic! Someone has to make her stop!" He looked directly at the mirror at last as he concluded, "Because we all just want to go home."

The reporter tilted the mirror toward himself. "You've seen it right here, folks. Heavy accusations from the unicorn known as Jeremy. Stay with us while we approach Lady Vell herself for her comments." Carrying the mirror, he marched toward the tower door.

Everyone who'd gathered to watch followed him.

"You did it!" Even told Jeremy.

"I know! I did! I really did! But . . . will it matter?"

Reaching the tower, the reporter pounded on Lady Vell's door. "*New City Mirror,* seeking a statement from Lady Vell on the accusations leveled against her."

The tower was silent.

The reporter banged on the door again. A few of the boarders flew themselves up to the higher windows. Even joined them, using her magic to rise up above the gardens.

Below, at last, the door opened. Even swooped down to

rejoin Odd and Jeremy as the centaur stepped outside. The crowd pressed closer, eager to hear his answer.

"Lady Vell is not available for comment," he boomed.

The reporter shoved the magic mirror at the centaur. "Can you tell us why Lady Vell doesn't care about the damage she has done?"

The centaur recoiled. "This is all inappropriate and unnecessary. Lady Vell cares deeply about the people of this land. Her actions are for the betterment of all."

"Not all!" Even yelled.

"We want to go home!" Odd shouted.

"The border magic belongs to everyone," Jeremy said. "It's not right for Lady Vell to take it!"

"Lady Vell is a genius," the centaur said. "Her work—"

"Her work took my home!" Jeremy said. "It's endangering mermaids and causing angry dragons and other dangerous creatures to wreak havoc on unprotected regions. And the problems will spread—things will get worse!"

"Your statement?" the reporter insisted.

The centaur retreated. He tried to shut the door, but the reporter wedged the mirror inside.

Suddenly, a whoosh of wind roared out through the door.

The curious crowd was pushed back.

Even fell, landing on a boy with a furry face and a squirrel tail. Scrambling to her feet, she rose onto her toes to see what was happening. Lady Vell stood in the doorway, filling it. The wind had pulled strands of hair out of her coif of screwdrivers and other tools. Her silk robe fluttered around her.

"Can I help you?" she asked.

The reporter scrambled to grab his magic mirror and prop it up. "What do you say to the allegations that your inventions have caused devastation along the border? Do you believe your work is more important than the well-being of those who live by the gateways? Did you know how much damage you were doing? Now that you do know, do you plan to stop using border magic?"

Lady Vell studied him and then the crowd. Last, she looked at Even and Odd.

"The public wants to know," the reporter persisted. "Will you let these children return to their parents? Will you return the magic you've taken and allow the gateways to reopen? Will you stop your activities in the face of the destruction you're causing?"

Even held her breath. They'd exposed the truth. Maybe Lady Vell would understand the importance of what was happening. People's lives were being affected. Damage was being done. Families were being split, homes lost. Now that Lady Vell knew for certain, and now that she knew that others knew and that soon the Academy of Magic would know . . . she had to stop!

Lady Vell held up her hand, and the crowd quieted.

Even stepped forward. "Will you stop? Please?" she asked.

"No," Lady Vell said.

And she threw her hands in the air. Fire spurted up around her tower, without touching any of the walls themselves. Even felt a blast of cold instead of heat. As the cold fire spread, the flames turned silver and encased the entire tower. The crowd gasped, retreating back through the gardens, all the way to the yellow brick road.

Lady Vell smiled, turned, and went inside.

The door sealed behind her, leaving a wall of silver fire, laced with blue bubbles.

15

THE SILVER-AND-BLUE FIRE burned without touching the trees or gardens. It didn't behave like an ordinary fire — it didn't spread, and it didn't give off heat. Even poked at the flames and then yelped as pain shot through her finger. She popped her finger into her mouth.

"Don't play with fire," Odd told her.

"Thanks." Even glared at her sister. Taking her finger out of her mouth, she looked at it, expecting to see it red and burned, but it looked fine. It throbbed for a few seconds more, then stopped. The magic fire hurt but didn't actually burn. Neither growing nor shrinking, the fire curled around Lady Vell's tower, making it look like a silver candle.

Eventually, once it was clear that no further excitement was going to happen, the group of boarders and the last of the wannabe boarders trickled away. The rabbit reporter had set-tled in to watch the tower, occasionally jotting down lines in a notebook or commenting to his magic mirror. Even, Odd, and Jeremy held out for another hour, as shadows grew across the estate, but when the sun began to set, they trudged back into the city.

"My parents are going to be so mad when they find out I was in the mundane world without permission. And it was all for nothing." Jeremy's head drooped, and even his horn seemed less sparkly.

"We had to try," Even told him. He'd shared the truth, and that had to make a difference, even if it wasn't one they could see yet. Right? She needed to believe that.

In the city, a few streetlights flickered as fairies flew between them, lighting them with a pinkish amber glow. Except for the abundance of tentacles and wings, it looked like any ordinary city as people drifted home for dinner.

Jeremy pointed his horn at the streetlights. "We shouldn't have stayed so long. It will be fully dark soon. I don't love the idea of traveling in the dark. Especially if there are any more displaced dragons out there."

"What choice do we have?" Even asked. "We don't have any place to stay. We have to go back. We'll just follow the road." As she said it, she wondered how that was going to be possible. It wasn't as if the unicorn had headlights. And the road was a mess, the farther you got from the city.

"You want to just give up and go back?" Odd asked. "Really?"

"I'm not giving up! I just don't know what to do next." She wished someone were here to tell her what to do. *Some hero I'll be,* she thought. If this was a test of her readiness, she'd failed miserably. She couldn't think of any way her so-called first quest could have gone worse. *I'm not ready for any of this.* "Maybe if we go back to Unicorn Hill, Jeremy's parents will have more ideas." Surely, there had to be someone more qualified than she was to fix all this.

"Let's at least eat before we head back," Jeremy said. "I can buy us food." He trotted across the street, to where one of the vendors was wheeling a cart. The vendor was a green-skinned genie with heavily muscled arms and smoke instead of legs. It looked like he sold roasted peanuts. And . . . were those dancing frogs? Squinting, Even thought the frogs were wearing top hats and dancing with canes. She saw the genie gesture, and a bale of hay appeared on the street beside the cart with a *poof.*

"Not horse food!" Odd called after him. "Human food!"

"And no cupcakes!" Even called.

"Definitely no cupcakes!" Odd agreed.

They watched Jeremy talk to the vendor. "Maybe the broad-cast worked, and a hero is already on their way," Even said. She had to think positive. The alternative was curling up into a ball and crying.

"What if the Academy didn't see it?" Odd asked. "Or what if

they *did* see it but don't care? What happens next? Who can—"
She cut off abruptly, and her eyes went wide. "Mom?"

Even turned and saw her: Mom! In her business suit and ironed blouse, with her hair pinned back, Mom was walking briskly down the street. Spotting them, she started running toward Even and Odd. They ran to her. "Mom!"

Odd threw herself into Mom's arms, and Mom squeezed her tight. Even wrapped her arms around both of them. "You're here!" Odd cried.

"How did you find us?" Even asked.

"You were broadcast everywhere," Mom said. "It was impossible not to know where you were. I went to Lady Vell's estate and then followed the road straight into the city—and here you are. But what are you doing here? You're supposed to be home! Why isn't your father with you? Is he all right? Are you all right?"

"We're all right, I promise," Odd said, hugging her again. Her voice was muffled by Mom's shirt. "Except for being stuck on the wrong side of the border."

"Your father shouldn't have allowed—" Mom began.

"It's not his fault," Even said. "It's mine. I thought we could test the portal, see Firoth, and pop back home and tell everyone that everything was fine."

"But everything wasn't fine," Odd said.

"You're right about that. It certainly isn't fine," Mom said.

We're in so much trouble, Even thought. She was supposed to be home, studying for the level-five exam, which she was supposed to take the day after tomorrow. Instead she and her sister were here, and it was her fault.

But Mom didn't yell at them. "Have you eaten anything? Where have you slept?" She examined them both as if they were crystal bowls that could have been chipped. When she didn't find any bruises or broken bones, she relaxed a bit.

"We spent last night with Jeremy's family in Lakeview," Odd said. She waved to Jeremy, and he trotted back to them, leaving the vendor and his cart without buying anything. "This is our friend Jeremy. He's been helping us. Jeremy, this is our mother!"

"You found her!" Jeremy said.

"She found us," Even said. "Mom, Jeremy's home switched places with a lake. And we saw a dragon just appear out of nowhere. But Lady Vell—"

"I heard what you said, every word, through the mirror," Mom said. "I've been in the border towns, trying to figure out what was going on. Every town near the border is experiencing effects, and I'd narrowed down the cause to a disturbance in the natural flow of border magic. But I lacked the final puzzle piece. I didn't imagine my daughters would be the ones to unravel this mystery."

"Is it true?" Odd asked. "Is it your power stone that Lady Vell is using?"

"She is, or was, a respected researcher," Mom said. "A scientist. We believed we were selling it to someone who would study it for academic purposes without using it. We thought she understood its dangers."

"A scientist who studies magic," Odd said. "Isn't that a contradiction?"

Mom gave a quick laugh, but Even thought it sounded strained. She tried not to imagine how freaked out Mom must have been to see them appear on a magic mirror. Any second now they were going to get a lecture on how irresponsibly they'd behaved and how she'd expected more from them. "Not at all," Mom answered Odd. "You can study magic just as you can study butterflies or volcanoes or a disease."

"Magic isn't a disease," Even said.

"But it *is* a natural force," Mom said. "Before your father and I started the border store, we researched the behavior of magical forces. When we discovered the consequences of using a power stone to manipulate those forces, we halted our research and issued warnings to the Academy of Magic."

Consequences, Even thought. *She means us.*

"We'll find a way to fix this," Mom said, hugging them again. "You two have already done so much, discovering the source of the problem. I will spread the word—there are a number of people I've been working with who are also concerned about what's happening in the borderlands. We'll contact the Academy and figure out what to do. Don't worry. For right now, let's get you some dinner and a nice place to sleep."

Even felt so full of relief that she wanted to cry. Mom was here! Mom knew what to do.

Jeremy cleared his throat, then looked at the sky as if he hadn't done it.

"Can our friend come with us?" Odd asked.

"Yes, of course," Mom said warmly. "Jeremy, thank you for helping our family. It's very nice to meet you."

One arm around Even and one arm around Odd, Mom led them to a domed building with an array of flowers outside. As they approached, the flowers took flight, and the flock of flower fairies flew to the next building and gathered around the entrance, framing it in an arch of biting blossoms. "I just took the house out of storage," Mom said. "It's dusty, but it will do. You may even remember it."

Even walked inside and halted as she faced a semicircle of purple Seuss-like trees inside a room that looked strangely familiar. Cobwebs clung to the arches, and thick dust obscured the mosaic floor. She knew without looking, though, that the floor was a scene of waves in an ocean in every color blue imaginable.

Odd joined her. "What is it?"

Walking slowly, Even touched the trunk of one of the trees. It shivered beneath her fingers, as if it recognized her, too. "I do remember this place."

"This used to be home," Mom said.

"Really?" Odd said.

Yes, really, Even thought, but she couldn't seem to make herself speak. Memories that she'd forgotten were flashing like photographs in her mind: *Eating breakfast around* . . . She ran forward and picked up the side of a fallen table, then pushed it back onto its legs. *Breakfast around this table.* "Whenever Dad made pancakes, he'd shape them like birds . . ."

"And I'd make them fly up to the trees," Mom said.

He'd stopped making them like birds when they'd moved to an ordinary house in Connecticut. Maybe because there weren't trees inside to fly them to.

"I didn't remember that the trees were inside." She tried to reconstruct her memory. The floor was a mosaic, and the walls were painted blue. She looked at the ceiling and saw a painting of stars, exactly as she expected.

"Sometimes we stretched hammocks between the trees," Mom said. "You liked to sleep here, even though you had a perfectly nice bedroom." She gestured at an archway that had suddenly appeared. A hallway sprouted off it — it hadn't been there a minute ago. The house was growing around them.

Odd joined them. "I don't remember any of this."

Mom hugged her shoulders. "You're a year younger. That can make the difference. It's why you've never thought of this world as home. You don't remember it that way."

"Home has Dad," Odd said.

"Indeed it does, sweetie," Mom said. "It certainly does. And we're going to get back to him soon. I promise." She hugged both of them again, and Even and Odd hugged her just as hard. Even breathed in the familiar smell of the soap Mom always used, and she felt, for the first time since meeting Lady Vell, that everything was going to be okay again. Her optimism crept back in.

Jeremy piped up. "Could we have dinner first? Please?"

Mom laughed. "Of course. I'll bring you some. Don't eat anything in the kitchen. Any food you find has been there so long it's probably alive now."

Even wasn't sure whether Mom was joking or not.

Mom asked Jeremy, "Any allergies?"

"No, ma'am," he said.

"Stay here, and no going through any portals to other worlds without me," Mom told them, and disappeared through the door.

Even was nearly sure Mom was joking that time.

They found chairs and arranged them around the table. Even pulled a tattered curtain off a window and used it to dust the tabletop, flying the rag by magic. Jeremy shook off his satchel and pushed it into a corner where it wouldn't be in the way.

"Do you think she's mad at us for coming here?" Even asked Odd quietly.

"She's relieved she found us," Odd said. "That will last until we're fed. Then she'll be mad. Or worried. Or both. Or maybe she won't. It's not like I've been in this situation before."

"Mom probably hasn't been either." But she was here! And she'd fix everything.

Even liked the idea of dumping all their problems into Mom's lap. Mom had been coming to the magic world for years, ever since they left it, *and* she was an expert in magical forces in general and the power stone in particular. She had to know a way to stop Lady Vell and restore the magic to the border. Mom had even said she knew people who could help. And she'd mentioned contacting the Academy.

Mom returned with several platters of food, as well as a bucket of oats. She levitated the bucket next to her and let it settle in front of Jeremy. He thanked her and then plunged his face into it. She put two plates with what looked like chicken and a pile of wilted spinach in front of Even and Odd. "You eat the greens," Mom said. "No argument."

Even poked at the vegetables with a fork. She probably would have loved them if she were still a skunk. She remembered she hadn't told Mom that part yet. *Might as well, while she's still feeling relived, not mad.* "I got stuck as a skunk. When the gateway closed, I wasn't able to work magic, even though it was an even day."

"Is your magic working normally now?"

Concentrating, Even pictured herself as a skunk. She felt her body shrink, fur fluff all over her, and a tail sprout from her behind. Finishing, she examined herself. It felt surprisingly normal to be a skunk again. Plus, that was the fastest transformation she'd ever done. Focusing, she imagined herself as human and shifted back. "All fine."

"Nice job," Mom said.

"FYI," Odd said, "we might have to air out the house when we get home. And the store. When" — she hesitated, as if afraid to ask — "do you think we'll be able to go home?" She held her breath as she waited for the answer.

"I'm working on it," Mom promised. "I've asked my colleagues to join us here — that was my original reason for bringing this house out of storage. We'll use it as a meeting place. Once we have all our facts in order, we'll reach out to the Academy of Magic for direction on how to handle Lady Vell. But I don't want you two to worry about it. You've done enough. Knowing that Lady Vell and the power stone are responsible . . . This changes everything."

She's not mad, Even thought. And then she thought, *Am I?* "There was something upsetting that happened. We heard a story. About us. About our magic."

Odd kicked her on the shin. "Now?"

"Yes, now. It's relevant. Lady Vell knew about it too. In fact, everyone seems to know about it except for us. Mom, did your and Dad's experiments cause us to share magic?"

Mom sat down heavily. She looked, for a moment, lost. It wasn't an expression that Even had ever seen on her face before. Mom was always in control. She was the one who knew everyone's schedules, who made sure everyone ate and had clean clothes, who made sure the shop opened on time and had all the supplies it needed. She took care of all of them, even Dad. *Who takes care of her?* Even wondered. But she set that question aside to think about later. Right now, Mom owed them some answers.

"You said we were born this way. But we weren't, were we?"

"You weren't," Mom said. She turned her attention to the table, as if the words were easier to say while not looking at her daughters. Plates, cups, and utensils floated out of a cabinet and set themselves down.

"I knew it!" Odd cried. "I was never meant to have magic. That's why it's always felt so weird and why I've always been so bad at it."

"You're bad at it because you don't practice," Mom said.

"That's what I tell her," Even said.

"And it *is* your magic," Mom said to Odd, looking over at her. "Even was born without magic. But you, Odd, were born with it."

Even felt her mouth drop open. *It's not my magic? I'm not magical?* But . . . it had always felt so right. She was the sister who loved magic, the one who dreamed of a future with magic. She was the one who planned on becoming a wizard and being a hero of Firoth . . . How could it not be her magic?

"That can't be," Odd said, echoing Even's thoughts as if she could read them. "Even's the one who loves magic! Not me."

"We were studying the power stone," Mom explained. "It was supposed to siphon magic from the earth itself and then share it, split between your father and me. Instead it siphoned magic from Odd, and it shared her magic between you two. We'd never even seen that as a possibility. We'd never imagined our work would touch either of you."

"Even could have taken it all," Odd said.

"You don't mean that," Mom said. "It's a part of you. You have magic. Just like you have your eyes and your smile."

But it's not supposed to be part of me, Even thought.

Concentrating, she lifted her fork into the air with her magic. She added the other utensils. They danced above the table. How could this magic not be hers? It felt like hers. But . . . it wasn't supposed to be? It was all Odd's?

"After the accident, we couldn't face continuing with our experiments, knowing that they could impact you," Mom said. "That was why we moved across the border and started over. Our failure . . . We wanted to give all of us a fresh start and new opportunities."

Even let the utensils fall lightly down on the table, like leaves from a tree. "You mean you didn't want to risk me accidentally stealing anything else from my sister."

"You didn't steal my magic," Odd said. "You *did* steal my favorite sweatshirt and spill ketchup on it. But this . . . you didn't do anything wrong."

"Odd is right," Mom said. She looked anxious, as if she expected Even and Odd to yell at her instead of the other way around. She'd never looked so uncertain. "Your father and I are to blame. And we are to blame for the way you found out. We should have told you."

"Why didn't you?" Even realized the room looked blurry because there were tears in her eyes. She wiped them away, refusing to cry. *I'm not magical. Not really.* She'd always defined herself as the sister who loved magic. It was her thing, the way that animals were Odd's thing. But now . . . *Who am I if I'm not magical?*

"At first we worried about how you'd react," Mom said. "But then we thought there was no reason for you to know. It can't be changed. You are who you are. I'm sorry that you found out from someone else. We should have told you. I'm sorry."

"It's fine," Odd said automatically. "I mean . . . well, I'm just glad you're here."

Even didn't feel "fine." Her thoughts were swirling. But Mom looked so anxious that she echoed Odd. "I'm glad you're here too."

"When the gateways closed, I feared I wouldn't ever see you again," Mom said. "Now that we're together and now that you've discovered the cause of the problem, I know anything's possible." She hugged them both tight.

"You think we'll find a way home?" Odd asked.

"I know we will," Mom said. "But first, eat and rest. You're welcome to stay the night as well, Jeremy. I'll send word to your family so they won't worry."

He lifted his head out of his bucket long enough to thank her again.

Mom's here, Even thought. *It's all going to be okay.*

But a little part of her wondered if she was ever going to feel okay again.

16

"WAIT," MOM SAID the next morning.

"Wait," she said in the afternoon.

"Wait," she said, every time Even or Odd asked if there was a plan or news or any progress with the Lady Vell situation at all.

In the meantime, new arrivals kept knocking on the door, and the house magically expanded. More rooms with more purple Seuss trees inside them budded off the main room. Even recognized some of the new magical beings, or at least knew of them—a centaur who said he was Frank's brother; Mr. Fratelli's daughter, and two of his cousins—but there were several more she hadn't heard of, whose homes had been displaced or who had family members stranded in the mundane world. The new arrivals brought their own food, and the table stretched longer. More hammocks were strung between more trees. As each visitor appeared, they met with Mom, conferring behind a closed door in a makeshift conference room. She seemed to know all of them.

And while the grownups met and talked and planned in hushed whispers, Even, Odd, and Jeremy waited. They watched the magic mirror and saw the rabbit reporter outside New City, highlighting the refugees fleeing the border regions.

At first, Even felt relief. The grownups were taking care of it. She'd done everything she could. But as the hours wore on, Even wished she was in the room where the discussions were happening. Sure, she hadn't won her junior medallion yet and was far from being ready for a hero's quest—she didn't even have magic today. Still, though, maybe there was some way she could help.

In the late afternoon, when Mom emerged, Even asked, "Mom, what can I do?"

"Even, look around," Mom said. "Everyone's busy. I know you're bored and worried you'll miss your level-five exam, but—"

Even hadn't thought about her exam in ages, though Mom was right: she was definitely going to miss it. She was surprised that the thought didn't upset her more. A few days ago, she would have said that passing the exam was the most important thing in her life. But now . . . "I mean, how can I help? Please, Mom, I know I'm not a wizard, but there has to be something useful I can do."

Softening, Mom kissed her on her forehead. "You're sweet to offer, but we're doing all we can. We've sent a full explanation of the Lady Vell situation to the Academy of Magic. Given the seriousness of all that's going on, they should expedite our petition to be granted a quest to handle the matter. With luck, our family will be reunited at home tomorrow, and all will be back to normal. But for now, I just need you to look after yourself and your sister while I help the new arrivals settle in. We have two more coming shortly."

Feeling even more useless, Even retreated to her bedroom—or at least the room she thought she remembered sharing with her sister. After all this time, it didn't feel like it was hers.

"You okay?" Odd asked her.

"Just worrying," Even said.

"Hey, that's my job."

Dredging up a smile, Even was about to reply when Jeremy raced into their room. "Can I stash this here?" he asked. Without waiting for an answer, he tossed his head, and the pink satchel sailed off and landed on Odd's bed. If it had been an even day, Even would have caught it with magic, but as it was, it thumped onto the downy mattress and sank between the pillows.

"What's wrong?" Odd asked.

"I don't want my cards and stuff confiscated," he said. "They can't take it if they can't find it. Consider it yours. I officially gift it to you, even the soda, though I already drank one of the cans so there are only five in there. You'll have to share one if you want to split them equally."

"Your parents are here?" Even guessed.

"Your mother invited them," Jeremy confirmed. "Apparently, they've been chatting by magic mirror ever since your mom first contacted them to tell them I was here with you." His nostrils flared.

"Do you think you're in trouble?" Odd asked.

"It'll be a miracle if I'm not."

Even had expected their mom to be furious with them, but she hadn't been at all. Just relieved they were okay. Maybe Jeremy would be wrong about how his parents would react too.

Leaving the satchel on the bed, she trailed after Odd as she followed Jeremy out to the main room, where Jeremy's parents waited. His mother and father were bathed in the late afternoon light that streamed in through the many skylights in the ceiling. Their horns reflected the warm glow.

"You, son, are hereby confined to Unicorn Hill for the next three months," Starry Delight said with the air and finality of a celestial judge.

Jeremy hung his head low, his horn dipping toward the floor.

"But you should also know we're proud of you," his father, Effervescent Spring, said in his deep, musical voice.

Jeremy raised his head.

"You have been helping those in need of help," Starry said. "Caring for those beyond yourself. Truthfully, we weren't certain you were capable of that kind of empathy—you've rarely shown it to your own kind—and this is a relief to see. You're still being punished for disobedience, but that's only for a specific infraction."

"You're here to bring me home?" Jeremy asked.

"Not yet," Spring said. "We are here to help. So many have been affected. There have been more and more reports up and down the border. You started something, Jeremy, with your magic-mirror broadcast. People have been coming forward and sharing their stories."

"Has it made any difference?" Even asked. "Is anyone doing anything about Lady Vell?"

Mom entered the room, and Even noticed how tired she looked, as if she hadn't slept since yesterday. *Maybe she hasn't,* Even thought. She knew Mom had been working hard to figure out the problem with the border even before she'd found them. But despite the exhaustion etched on her face, Mom was smiling. "Starry Delight," Mom greeted Jeremy's parents, "Effervescent Spring. Lovely to meet you in person. I'm afraid we're still waiting for the Academy of Magic."

"Still?" Odd cried.

"They've been inundated with emergencies," Mom said. "Griffins were stranded on an island when their home was displaced. A sea monster had to be extracted from a river. There are dragon sightings up and down the borderlands . . . There's reportedly a lot of disagreement within the Academy over how to handle the situation—politics, you know, and the weight of bureaucracy. The Academy is not as nimble as it once was."

The unicorns nodded knowingly.

"I'm certain that as soon as the immediate crises are resolved, they'll have a decision for us on how to proceed." Mom smiled at all of them, and Even wondered if anyone else could tell how strained that smile was.

She doesn't know what the Academy is going to say, or when they're going to say it, Even realized. *She's waiting just like we are.*

A terrible thought tiptoed into her mind: What if the grownups didn't know what to do?

★★★

There was no decision by morning.

Even tried to distract herself from worrying by practicing her magic. She transformed into a rabbit, a hamster, a cat, and a panda in rapid succession, and then she levitated herself so she could pace on the ceiling. As she practiced, she thought about the fact that this magic wasn't really hers, or wasn't supposed to be hers. But even knowing that, it still *felt* like hers. It worked exactly the same as it always had.

Sitting on the floor, Odd and Jeremy were playing Farmcats.

Upside down, Even walked above them before transforming into a flamingo. Her wing beats rustled their cards.

"Are you going to stop anytime soon?" Odd asked.

"As soon as this is over," Even said, changing back to herself.

"You could play with us," Jeremy offered. "It would pass the time." He flipped a card over with his teeth and then scooted it forward with his horn. "Rooster wakes your Maine Coon for ten points."

Odd laid down a card. "Interrupting with a Tractor."

"No, thanks," Even said. She resumed pacing the ceiling. After a while, she switched to pacing on the walls.

Mom barely came out of the conference room, and when she did, she looked so distracted and worried that Even didn't want to ask how it was going.

Eventually, she agreed to play Farmcats, and she spent the afternoon losing every match.

★★★

Mom woke them shortly after dawn the next day, an odd day. "Get dressed," she told them. "There's progress. We just received word that the Academy of Magic has approved our quest to remove the power stone from Lady Vell's possession."

"That's great!" Odd said. "What does that mean?"

"It means you only have to be patient a little longer. This will all be over soon. We have formed a team of accredited wizards, myself included, to take the power stone away from her. Once the stone is deactivated, all the magic she's hoarded should flow back into the border. She won't be able to hurt the borderlands anymore, and we'll be able to go home."

Jumping out of her hammock bed, Even dressed. So did Odd. "Why did it take the Academy so long to say yes?" Even asked.

"It's run by committee," Mom said. "And there's a lot of paperwork. But the important thing is that we got the go-ahead, and now we need your help."

"Yes!" Even cheered.

"What kind of help?" Odd asked.

"You have seen the inside of Lady Vell's workshop. We need you two and Jeremy to tell us everything you saw, especially as it relates to the protections around the power stone." Mom guided them into the room where she'd been meeting with the newcomers. A dozen creatures and people were waiting there: Jeremy's parents, two centaurs, one three-headed dog, humans, a mouse with a sword strapped to her waist, a turtle with a many-colored shell, a two-foot-tall griffin . . . Several of them were chewing on their breakfasts. Some looked as if they'd just woken up. Others, like Mom, looked as if they'd never slept. Even recognized Joj, the goblin from Lakeview.

"Are your mermaids okay?" Even asked.

"They will be," Joj said, "once all this is fixed."

Odd asked, "But if you're here, who's feeding them?"

"Hired a local elf with the last of my gold. They've enough fish to last a couple of days. After that . . . Gotta fix this mess."

Jeremy joined them, whispering, "What's going on?"

Even whispered back, "Mom said we could help."

Odd hung back behind Even, as adults of various shapes and sizes all turned to stare at them. Mom stepped forward. "These are my children, Even and Odd, and their friend Jeremy. They've been within Lady Vell's tower and have information that could help us in our quest. Tell us what you saw."

For an instant, Even imagined herself at the head of an army of magical beings, leading the charge on the silver tower, and then she shook herself as she realized everyone was waiting for them to talk. She began. "Well, first there's the wall of silver fire around the tower."

"We know about that!" the mouse called.

"Everybody knows about that," Joj said. "It was on every mirror."

Even swallowed. "It wasn't there when we first visited. The centaur let us in, and the door locked behind us." She felt them all staring at her, and her throat dried up.

"The door has lots of locks, around the sides and top," Odd volunteered.

Even nodded. Together, she and Odd described the main room, how its ceiling went up to the peak of the tower, how the room was filled with tables that overflowed with Lady Vell's inventions, how there was a massive vat of blue bubbling liquid in the center of the room —

"That liquid contains the stolen magic," Effervescent Spring said. "Once we separate the vat from the power stone, all the magic should flow back to its original source, like a dam opening to release a river."

"It's connected to the power stone by a tube, which leads from the vat to a pedestal," Even said. "She keeps the pedestal with the stone inside a giant bubble. She said it's protected against all magic. I guess the bubble is some kind of shield?" She described what the bubble looked like and its size, with Odd adding comments.

Jeremy stepped up to contribute what he'd observed. He'd paid a lot of attention to her half-finished inventions, and he described where they were in the room, in relation to the vat of blue bubbly magic.

"Are there any other protections?" a cat asked. "Tripwires? Booby traps? Guards? Guard dogs? Guard dragons? Iron portcullis? Forest of thorns? Skeleton army?"

The interrogation continued for another hour, as the adults drew out every little detail that the sisters and Jeremy could remember. By the end, Even felt exhausted.

Mom shooed them back into their room and kissed Even and Odd. "You did wonderfully."

"We can help more," Even said. "We can be your guides."

She glanced at Odd and was relieved to see her nodding vigor-ously. She wanted to help too. Maybe neither of them was ready to be a hero, but there had to be something they could do to *help* the heroes.

"You'll stay here."

More waiting. More worrying.

"But maybe we could—"

Mom gave her a look. "Even." The name said everything: *I'm not discussing this anymore. My decision is final. You'll stay here because I said so, and I'm your mother.* It wasn't the kind of look or tone that you argued with.

"How are you going to get inside?" Odd asked. "It's sur-rounded by that silver fire."

"We have many high-powered magic users among us," Mom said. "Don't you worry about that." She patted Odd's head. "Remember, five things to be grateful for: we're together, we know the cause of the problem, the Academy has approved us to take action, she's only one person, and we are resourceful." She smiled reassuringly at both of them. "We'll be home with your father by the end of the day. You can count on that."

***

Soon after, while it was still early morning and most of the city still slept, Mom and the dozen magical beings who'd pledged to help her were assembled in the main room with the purple trees. Of them, only Joj was staying behind—along with Even,

Odd, and Jeremy, of course, who were left behind because their parents insisted on it, for their safety. Joj remained at the house as backup.

"Give us two hours," Mom told Joj. "If we aren't back by then, contact the Academy of Magic and tell them they need to send more wizards."

"Yes, ma'am," Joj said.

Odd overheard and yelped. "What do you mean if you're not back? Of course you're going to come back! Why wouldn't you come back?"

"Mom's definitely coming back," Even said firmly. "She's just trying to be extra safe and think of everything. Right, Mom?"

"That's right, sweetheart," Mom said reassuringly. "This shouldn't take long, and we'll be home with your father before you know it. Maybe even earlier."

"Can't they send the police? Or the army?" Odd asked.

"The Academy of Magic is sending *us*," Mom said.

"But you run a store!" Odd said. "Why you?"

"Because I care," Mom said. "And because I didn't always run a store. I'm an accredited wizard and an expert on exactly the kind of magic that Lady Vell is using. Please don't worry. I promise I'm going to take care of everything. Stay here, and stay safe. I'll be back soon."

She hugged and kissed them both, and Even and Odd squeezed side by side in the doorway to watch the unicorns and magic users head down the still mostly empty street. Jeremy stuck his head out between them to watch too.

Once they were out of sight, the sisters and the unicorn returned inside to begin waiting.

★★★

One hour later, the grownups hadn't returned.

"I can't stand this," Odd said.

"It's the not knowing," Even agreed. "They should have let us come."

"I, for one, am just as happy to not go near a heavily fortified wizard tower," Jeremy said. "How about another game of Farmcats?"

"I can't concentrate enough to do anything," Odd said. "Not even play Farmcats."

"Afraid of my Tractor card?" he teased.

"You can't use a Tractor if you don't draw a Farmer. But no, this isn't the time."

Even tried not to imagine all the ways things could go wrong. They might have failed to get inside the tower. They might have met with resistance—a wizard battle with Lady Vell.

"I want to check on them," Even said.

"You'll be caught," Odd said. "It's not an even day."

Odd was right. If it were an even day, she could have changed into a skunk and followed them, unseen. "I could just see if they've made it inside?" She wasn't suggesting that she charge in. Just . . . check if everything was okay. And then . . . well, she wasn't sure what she'd do, but there had to be *something*.

"You might mess up whatever they have planned," Odd said.

She was right, again. Without knowing what was going on at Lady Vell's tower, Even could make it worse by bumbling in. Their only option was to wait.

But she couldn't help picturing all the things that could have gone wrong. Her optimism couldn't compete with her imagination, and Even couldn't think of five things to be grateful for. All she could do was wonder:

What was happening in that tower?

Why weren't they back?

And what could she do about it?

★★★

At the end of three hours, the grownups still hadn't returned.

And Even was done with waiting.

17

EVEN SAID OUT loud what they'd all been thinking:

"They aren't back."

"I know," Odd said. "What do we do?"

"Joj has to contact the Academy of Magic, like Mom said. And they'll send more wizards to disable the power stone and rescue our mom and Jeremy's parents." That was the sensible course of action. She strode through the house, with Odd and Jeremy following.

They found Joj beneath the purple trees. He was shoving a wad of socks into a full backpack. *What's he doing?* Even wondered. "Joj, it's been over two hours, and they're not back. That means something must have gone wrong."

He waved a hand at a magic mirror. "Yeah, I'd say so."

All of them turned to look at the mirror. The rabbit reporter was back in front of Lady Vell's tower on her estate. The silver fire was laced with blue streaks, and it looked thicker than before. It was hard to see the door through the protective shield.

"The rabbit said they went in but didn't come out," Joj said.

Even stared at the image of the tower. *Mom's inside!*

"You have to tell the Academy of Magic," Odd said, panic in her voice.

Joj kept packing. "I already sent word. They don't have any more wizards to send. Everyone is overwhelmed—a flock of harpies showed up away from their territory and have been terrorizing the countryside. And a hydra was spotted in a forest of sprites an hour ago. Not to mention all sorts of innocent creatures have been transported away from home and need help getting back where they belong."

"But . . . Lady Vell is the source of the problems," Even said. "If they stop her, they stop all of this!"

"The Academy is great at talking big about heroic quests, but they aren't fast or efficient. Bureaucracy, you know? It will take them a while to agree on what to do next and even longer to actually do it."

Even thought of how long it had taken to just get permission for Mom and the others to handle Lady Vell, and they'd already been here, willing and ready. "Mom said to tell them to take emergency measures!"

"I don't think you understand how large Firoth is and how

many different kinds of beings live in careful balance," Joj said. "The border stretches for hundreds of miles, and there are problems along all of it—they told me they're facing a series of cascading emergencies."

Odd pointed to Joj's backpack. "Why are you packing?"

"Gotta go back to my lake," Joj said. "If this mess isn't going to be resolved fast, then I have to evacuate the mermaids. Won't be easy, but I've got a responsibility. Can't expect anyone else to do it for me."

"But you can't just leave us!" Odd said.

"Sorry, kid, but I have to," Joj said.

"You're just running away?" Even said. She couldn't believe what she was hearing. They couldn't just give up! Nothing had been solved!

"I'm running *toward*, not away," Joj said. "Wish I could do more here, but it looks like it's going to get worse before it gets better, and there are innocent people who need help whom I can actually do something for."

"If Lady Vell is stopped, it will help everyone," Even said. It seemed so clear to her: Stop Lady Vell and there wouldn't be any more emergencies. *Then* go fix the individual problems.

"I know that," Joj said. "But who's going to do it? The Academy isn't going to send anyone soon—they're just too slow. And there's no one left here. I'm no hero. I'm not equipped to go up against Lady Vell. If your mother and the others couldn't do it . . . No, I have to help whom I can, where I can. It's the best I can do."

"How long until the Academy of Magic sends help?" Odd asked. "I mean, you said it won't be soon, but do you mean 'not soon' as in 'not today' or 'not soon' as in 'not for days'?"

Joj shrugged. "No idea. It's chaos out there."

"We can't just wait and hope!" Even shouted. She'd tried that, again and again, but the only time anything moved forward was when they *did* something.

Unable to meet her eyes, Joj patted her shoulder awkwardly. "Keep your head down, and don't get yourselves into trouble. Be grateful you have a place to stay. There are going to be a lot of refugees coming into the city who won't have that." And with that, he left.

Even and Odd watched him go, while Jeremy paced behind them. The house suddenly felt very quiet and empty. Even felt as if her heart were beating louder than any other noise. She clenched and unclenched her fists as she tried to make herself think logically.

The grownups had clearly failed to stop Lady Vell. The Academy of Magic was useless.

So who was going to do it?

Can't expect anyone else to do it for me, Joj had said. But that was exactly what Even had been doing: expecting the unicorns to fix everything, expecting Lady Vell to help, expecting the Academy to save everyone, expecting Mom . . . She'd been waiting for a hero to come save the day.

Waiting in vain.

Chewing on her fingernails, Odd paced back and forth. "What if the border never reopens and we can never go home? What if Mom doesn't come back? What if—"

"Deep breath," Even told her.

"I can't think of anything I'm grateful for," Odd said.

"I'm grateful you're with me." Even squeezed her sister's hand. "And I'm grateful we're here."

"How can you say that?" Odd said. "The second thing, I mean. The first thing is nice. But I wish we were home. I wish we'd never stepped through the gateway."

"If we weren't here, then we wouldn't know that Mom went in that tower." Even pointed to the magic mirror, with the image of the tower swirling in blue-and-silver fire. She did not mention that if they hadn't been there, Mom wouldn't have known to go in at all . . . "We wouldn't even know she was in trouble. And we wouldn't have the chance to save her." As she said the words, she felt a weird kind of calmness spread through her. *No more waiting,* she thought.

"Us? Save her?"

"Yes, us," Even said. "If no heroes are going to show up, we'll have to do it ourselves."

"This is not the time for your stupid optimism," Odd said.

"This is *exactly* the time for stupid optimism. What do you want to do? Say 'Guess we'll never see our parents and home again—oh well, it was nice having a family while it lasted'?"

Odd glared at her. "Obviously not."

Even made her voice sound firm, as if she knew what she was doing. "The goblin made it pretty clear that the grownups aren't going to—or maybe can't—do anything. So who does that leave? Us."

"What are *we* supposed to do?" Jeremy said. "Knock on Lady Vell's door and say, 'Can we please have our parents back?' She's definitely not welcoming visitors now."

Maybe Even wasn't a hero yet. She wasn't ready for her own quest, or even to pass the exam she'd just missed. But she was done with waiting and worrying and hoping. "She welcomed us before."

"Yeah, because she wanted to use us," Odd said.

A plan was forming in her mind. It wasn't a plan that Odd would like. Or Mom and Dad. But Even liked it. "What if we let her?"

"Excuse me?" Odd said.

"I have an idea," Even said. "And it starts with knocking on that door."

"You mean the one wreathed in magical fire?" Jeremy asked.

"Yep. Come on. I'll tell you when we get there."

Even and Odd crept out of the house. Exactly who would catch them and stop them, Even didn't know, since Mom was missing, Dad was in another world, and Joj had fled, but it seemed like the thing to do. Jeremy tiptoed on his silver-white hooves behind them.

Despite everything that was going on, the street looked normal. Or as normal as a street could be when half the pedestrians flew by either magic or wings and most of the people didn't even look human. "Act casual."

Jeremy nodded to vendors as they strolled by. "Hey. What's up?"

"Shush," Odd told him. "You're being weird."

"I'm being myself."

"Be yourself less," Odd said.

"That's the worst self-help advice ever."

Even laughed louder than the joke deserved, trying to look as if they weren't on a secret mission to stop a megalomaniacal wizard. *Just chatter. Nothing to see here. Move along.* They had to keep it casual, she thought, at least until they were out of the city.

"So what's the plan?" Odd asked in a whisper.

"We're all going to do what we're good at," Even said.

Odd snorted. "And what's that? I'm terrible at magic. You don't have any magic today. And all Jeremy can do is poop cupcakes and tell the truth." To Jeremy, Odd added, "No offense."

"None taken," Jeremy said. "I'm a unicorn, not a wizard."

"We're not exactly a crack team of heroes," Odd said.

True. Real heroes should have been rescuing Mom, not the three of them. *But there's only us,* Even thought. *So we'll have to do.* "Stop imagining the worst."

"This *is* the worst," Odd said. "I don't have to imagine anything at all."

Outside Lady Vell's estate, beyond the tree-lined entrance, they halted and stared. The magic fire had indeed grown. It shone brighter than a spotlight and was sparking like an endless firework. Even wondered what had happened inside. Was Mom okay? Had she been hurt?

"Say Lady Vell does let us in, how are we supposed to rescue everyone?" Odd asked.

"We're going after the stone," Even said. "It's the only thing that will stop all of this."

"Mom and the others tried to take the stone. And they didn't come back."

"We aren't going to try to *take* it," Even said. She tried to sound as confident as possible: "We're going to destroy it. Or, specifically, I am."

The others stared at her.

She showed them Jeremy's satchel, which she was carrying slung over her shoulder. "That's why I brought this." Even reached in and pulled out the invisibility cloak. Her fingers disappeared into the folds as she shook it out.

"We can do this," Even told the others.

I hope, she added silently.

"First, we need to get inside . . ."

18

'EVEN WAS SWEATING beneath Jeremy's invisibility cloak. Made of thick wool, it felt like the itchiest sweater imaginable. Also, with the hood pulled up, it made it hard to see anything that wasn't directly in front of her. She trailed behind Odd and Jeremy.

Am I ready for this? she asked herself.

That had an easy answer: *No.*

She didn't have magic today, and even when she did, she wasn't a match for Lady Vell, a full-grown wizard. But it no longer mattered whether she was ready or not. *We have to try,* she thought. *And we have to try now.* They had no way of knowing what had become of Mom and the others. All they knew was they hadn't come out. Anything could have happened, or could be happening, within that silver tower. And there was no one else to deal with it.

Crossing through the gardens of Lady Vell's estate, she felt weirdly exposed, even though she knew she was invisible. The gardens were empty of boarders and wannabe boarders this time. The rabbit reporter was absent too—he must have moved on to reporting elsewhere. Maybe he was with the refugees again. Regardless, there was no one to stop them or even look curiously at them, as far as she could tell.

Ahead was the tower, wreathed in magic fire.

They stopped in front of the door.

"Okay," Even whispered. "Everyone set?" She wished she were anywhere else, but she wasn't going to say that out loud. They'd already discussed the plan, making sure each of them knew what to do.

"I hate this plan," Odd said.

"I kind of like it," Jeremy said.

"Thanks, Jeremy," Even whispered, surprised.

"I mean, it's doomed to fail. Probably won't even make it past the front door. Certainly won't outwit Lady Vell, and I'm definitely going to make a mess of it. But it will be fun until it all goes to pieces."

"Remember, all you have to do is be you," Even said. "And Odd . . ."

"I know what I need to do," she said.

Odd marched up to the door. It was coated in sparkling blue, so she didn't try to touch it. Instead she projected her voice, making it as loud as she could with as much magic as she could muster. She wasn't particularly good at it, and her voice buzzed like it was being broadcast from an out-of-range radio station. "Lady Vell? It's Odd Berry. I'm here to take you up on your offer!"

They waited.

Jeremy shifted from hoof to hoof.

Odd fidgeted with her hands, accidentally causing a watering can to rise in the air, spin in a somersault, and then crash down, spilling on the stones of the plaza. A pixie fluttered over and slurped up the puddle.

And Even continued to sweat beneath the cloak as she worried about all the things that could go wrong, starting with the centaur refusing to open the door. Their attempt could be very short.

It was easy to think positive when you were dreaming up a plan. Much harder when you were faced with reality.

Odd shouted again. "Lady Vell? Please, I'll do what you want! I'll say whatever you want to a mirror or the Academy of Magic or whoever!"

The air in front of them shivered, and the sparkling flames flashed blue and separated as if the fire were window curtains. With a *whoosh* noise, the wide door slid open. The centaur stuck his head out. "Repeat yourself."

"Please tell Lady Vell that I'm here to cooperate," Odd said, dropping the projection so that her voice sounded normal again.

"I'll say whatever she wants, if she lets my mother and Jeremy's parents and their friends go free."

Sparing a glance at Jeremy, the centaur scanned the grounds. "Where's your sister?"

"She doesn't know I'm here," Odd said. "Isn't one of us better than neither of us?"

"Humph. Just you. Not him," the centaur said, gesturing toward Jeremy. He opened the door a few inches so that Odd could enter, if she squeezed herself through. Even tried to peer past him to see if Lady Vell was waiting, but the centaur's bulk blocked her view.

Stepping forward, Jeremy said, "I want to see Lady Vell too."

The centaur snorted. "Lady Vell doesn't want to see you."

"I'd feel better if he were with me," Odd said quickly.

Even didn't expect it to work, but it was worth a try. They needed the door to open wider if Even was going to slip inside without the centaur noticing. She could *try* walking through with Odd, but her chances were better if Jeremy was entering as well, with his loud bell-like hooves and wide body to block any hint of her passage.

"Lady Vell isn't interested in your feelings, only your cooperation," the centaur said.

"Great! Then we'll cooperate together!" Jeremy said, and, without waiting for an answer, barged inside. He shoved past the centaur.

Shouting, the centaur hurried after him. "Get back here!"

Jeremy galloped down the hallway. "No, thank yoooou!"

Even scooted inside.

Odd followed Jeremy and the centaur into the hallway, while Even crept behind her, trying to match Odd's footsteps so that she wouldn't make any extra sound. When Odd halted just inside the workroom, Even did too and only narrowly kept herself from gasping as loudly as Odd did.

Lady Vell's laboratory looked as if it had been attacked by a jungle. Vines draped across the tables, and thick, thorny clumps filled a quarter of the room. In tangled masses, the vines had climbed the smooth walls to the glowing pinnacle of the roof, obscuring the light so that the whole workroom was bathed in a sickly green. Worse, though, they surrounded the vat of stolen magic, as well as the pedestal that held the power stone.

The power stone was hidden behind a thick wall of thorns.

Only just barely ahead of the centaur, Jeremy had reached the boards. "Ooh, can I try one of these? Yes?" He didn't wait for any kind of answer. "Great!" Leaping onto one, he rode it over the workroom tables and the cluster of vines. He sailed above the head of the centaur. "Wheeeeeeeeee!"

It had been Odd's idea to have Jeremy serve as a distraction. They'd left it up to him to decide how he was going to do it. *He's doing it,* Even thought. *Now it's my turn.*

"Good luck," Odd murmured.

"You too," Even whispered. She slipped away, skirting the edge of the room as the centaur chased after the unicorn.

Jeremy dodged and weaved and flew between the tables and the vines. He swooped into the air with the sparkling birds. Chasing him, the birds pecked at him, and he whinnied.

Pretending to object to his actions, Odd called, "Come back, Jeremy!" To the centaur, she said, "I'm so sorry. I had no idea he'd behave like this."

"Wheeeeeeeeeeeeeeeeeeeeeeeeeeeeee!"

"*Enough!*"

Even froze as the familiar voice rang out.

Lady Vell swept into the workroom and flicked her wrist, and Jeremy was whooshed off the board and tossed onto a table covered in vines. The vines immediately wrapped around him. He was hoisted into the air.

"Put me down! Ahhhh! Let me go! Get these things off me!" He flailed and squirmed as the vines lifted him higher.

"Let him go!" Odd cried.

Peering out from beneath the hood, Even wondered if the others were trapped under the vines too. Was Mom inside that tangle somewhere? She scanned the room, looking for bulges in the mass of greenery spilling across the massive room — there, and there . . . and could she see a hoof? Yes, there! That was either Starry Delight or Effervescent Spring, which meant that Mom could be cocooned in vines nearby too, as well as everyone else.

Please be okay in there, she thought.

The vines didn't seem to be hurting Jeremy. Just keeping him from escaping. She hoped the same was true for Mom and everyone else. If so . . . then all she needed to do was get the stone away from Lady Vell, rescue them, and save the day. *No pressure,* she thought.

Hands on her hips, Lady Vell demanded, "What is going on?"

"Don't blame Odd!" Jeremy said. He swung in a circle, pawing at the vines with his hooves. They wrapped more thickly around his torso. "She didn't do anything wrong!" That was true. She'd been innocently watching his antics from afar.

"He was trying to steal from you," the centaur said.

"Borrow," Jeremy corrected. "Taking with the intent to return is borrowing. And Odd didn't know I was planning to do that. You know I can't lie." Also true. They hadn't told him *how* to cause a distraction. Just to cause one.

"That is so." Lady Vell contemplated Odd. "Unicorn boy, tell me why Odd is here."

"She wants you to free her mother," Jeremy said.

Odd nodded enthusiastically.

"And she will really cooperate with me if I agree?" Lady Vell asked.

"You should talk to her," Jeremy advised, as he swung from the vines. "Hey, this is a little uncomfortable. Could you have the vines set me down?"

"I will cooperate," Odd said quickly. "I'll say whatever you want to your magic mirror if you'll let the people you captured, including Jeremy, go."

"I was asking the one I know cannot lie," Lady Vell said.

"She'll do it," Jeremy said. "She'll say whatever you want to your mirror if you'll free everyone." Again, the truth. Odd really would cooperate if it meant freeing everyone. It was an excellent backup plan. *It's just not the only plan,* Even thought, as she continued to silently inch around the workroom. She was careful not to step near any stray vines.

"Delightful," Lady Vell said.

"Now can I come down?" Jeremy asked.

"I want you to stay up there while you think about your life choices." Lady Vell wrapped her arm around Odd's shoulders. "Odd and I have to write a little speech. Things are delicate, and I don't want any improvising." She led Odd across the workroom toward the solarium. "Really, I am not a bad person. You must understand that. I didn't plan to capture anyone. It's not my fault they were breaking into my home with the intent of stealing my belongings and thereby triggered my protections. If we can come to a peaceful solution, that would be best for everyone. You're a wise girl to realize that."

They disappeared into the solarium while the centaur returned to the door, again taking up his position as guard. Jeremy swung slowly, suspended by vines.

My turn, Even thought.

Cloak tight around her, she kept an eye out for the centaur. She circled the vat, then stopped in front of where she knew the power stone was, behind the wall of thorns. The mass of greenery here was so dense that it was impossible to see through, but she could *feel* that it was there.

She pushed aside the vines—

And they writhed, wreathing themselves into a solid wall. It looked like snakes squirming together. She tried to pry them apart, and they tightened.

You can do this, she told herself.

She wasn't trying to overpower Lady Vell's vines with magic, after all, or hack them down by sheer muscle power, like Sleeping Beauty's prince. Even reached into Jeremy's satchel and drew out a can of soda. She shook it hard. *Here we go,* she thought.

Opening it, she aimed it at the wall of thorns.

Soda sprayed out, and the vines quit moving and lay limp. She pried them apart, and this time they stayed apart. She made a hole in the greenery and climbed through. Thorns snagged her cloak. She yanked it free. It ripped with a *snick,* but she kept it tight against her.

She readied a second can, shaking it hard. She only had five —Jeremy had drunk one. She hoped five was enough. She didn't know how thick the thorny vines were.

Using a second can, Even de-magicked another clump of writhing vines. She pushed through and burst out the other side. But instead of facing the pedestal, she found herself in front of a wall of fire.

Unlike the cold silver fire that surrounded the tower, this fire was a deep purple and hot. She didn't smell any smoke, but she could feel the heat of the fire, toasting her face. Sweat dribbled down her back. She saw the pedestal beyond it, through the haze.

She didn't let herself feel doubt. She'd come this far, and the only option was to keep going forward. Jeremy was trapped, along with Mom and everyone else, and Odd was with Lady Vell. *They're all depending on me,* Even thought.

Aiming a third can of soda, she sprayed it at the fire.

The purple flames hissed, and she sprayed the soda in an oval. As soon as it was wide enough for her, she hurried through. A corner of her cloak brushed the flames, and fire spread across the fabric.

Even tore the cloak off and stomped on it.

The fire went out.

She picked up the remnants of the cloak. The fire had consumed it unnaturally fast, and all that remained were a few tattered shreds. No more invisibility. She guessed Jeremy wasn't going to be returning it to its owner after all. She sent him a silent apology.

At last she faced the shimmer of the protective bubble around the power stone. Through it, the power stone was sparking like before, and with each spark, more blue bubbling liquid traveled from the stone, through the pipe, and into the vat. She was down to the final shield.

She took a step toward the bubble and hoped she was right about this. She only had two cans left. If this didn't work . . . *Think positive,* she reminded herself.

"I wuv you."

"I love you too," Even said without thinking.

Wait. Who said that?

She turned to see the creepy dolls waddling toward her, crawling beneath the remaining thorns. The fire hadn't returned where she'd quenched it. She froze — only for a second, but the dolls were moving fast. Quickly, they surrounded her. She shot a look at the stone beyond the bubble.

Only two cans left.

A doll began to climb up her leg. She shook it off as two leaped up to cling to her arm. "I wuv you!" they chanted.

Kicking at the dolls as if she were playing soccer, Even knocked them away. As they grabbed at her, she shook her second-to-last can. She sprayed it, and the dolls collapsed, limp, as the soda touched them.

More kept marching toward her, though.

Clutching the final can, she threw herself toward the pedestal. *Please work! Please . . . I'm not magic. Let me past!*

She burst through the bubble.

The magic-infused dolls thumped against it, unable to pass.

Catching her breath, Even faced the power stone. Only one can. One chance. She hoped this worked.

And then Lady Vell shouted, "Stop!"

19

"DO NOT MOVE," Lady Vell barked at Even.

At her command, the wall of purple fire vanished, and the vines receded.

Even shook the can of soda as hard as she could as Lady Vell stalked toward her through the shriveled thorns. Blue sparkles rained down on her, sizzling as they hit the greenery.

Where's Odd?

"I will not allow you to steal my life's work!"

"I'm not going to steal anything." *Unlike you,* she added silently. "I'm just . . . drinking a nice carbonated beverage while I wait for my sister to finish talking with you. Is she done? Because once she is, we'd like to go home." She hoped her voice didn't sound as shaky as she felt.

"Your sister is with my other unwelcome guests."

Even wanted to open the soda right now, before Lady Vell

came any closer, but she also had to make certain her sister was unhurt. "You said you'd free them if she cooperated. Did she cooperate?"

"Yes, but she also allowed that pesky unicorn to wreak havoc in my laboratory—"

"You agreed to set everyone free if she cooperated. I heard you. Did you hurt her?" Her heart was pounding hard as she asked.

"Of course not," Lady Vell said. "I'm not a monster."

"You've kept us from Dad. You've torn people's homes apart. Explain to me how you're not a monster?"

Lady Vell gestured toward her inventions. "Look at all I've done! And these are only the beginning. A proof of concept that I can make magic available to everyone. These are equalizers. All I want is to improve the lives of the people who were born without magic. Surely, you of all people can understand that."

The terrible thing was that Even *did* understand that. If her parents hadn't used the power stone, then she wouldn't even have magic every other day. She would be without magic, the kind of person that Lady Vell said she wanted to help.

But this was *not* the way to help anyone.

And not everyone without magic needed help. Odd had never wanted magic, even though it had been hers to begin with. She'd have been perfectly happy to be magicless her whole life. What Lady Vell was doing was reckless and dangerous. She acted without any care for consequences, as if she and only she knew what was best for everyone.

She had to stop. *Or be stopped.*

"Step away from the power stone," Lady Vell said.

"If I leave the stone alone, what will you do?" Even said. "Are you going to free everyone? Are you going to stop using the stone to drain the border magic? Are you going to let people have their homes back and return to their families? Or are you going to keep not caring about who you hurt?"

"You can't keep the stone from doing its work," Lady Vell said. "A power stone is rare and powerful. You don't possess any magic that can counter it. Indeed, today you do not possess any magic at all."

"Maybe I don't need magic for this." Even shook the soda again.

Quickly, Lady Vell said, "If you destroy the power stone, I can't use it to help you and your sister."

"We don't need your help."

"You do," Lady Vell said. "You need someone who has studied the power stone. Someone who knows how it works, and someone who can use that knowledge to give both you and your sister what you've always craved."

"I don't want anything from you," Even said.

"I can make it so you have all the magic and Odd has none," Lady Vell said, "if that's what the two of you want."

Fingers on the soda-can tab, Even froze. "You can do that?"

"Easily," Lady Vell said. "I know how to properly control the power stone. Look at me. I don't have magic naturally. All I have is thanks to the power stone." She waved at the vines, the doors, the magical birds flying above them. "I know how to transfer magic from your sister to you. You could both have the lives you yearn for."

That . . . was what Even had always wanted.

And what Odd had always wanted.

Odd would be able to be ordinary all the time. She wouldn't have to pretend she didn't have magic. And Even would never have to do without magic.

She'd be able to practice every day. She'd win her medallion, and no one would ever be able to say she didn't deserve it. She could become a hero of Firoth and be able to do great things — important things that would help people who needed help. She tightened her grip on the soda can. "I don't know . . ."

"My work has to continue," Lady Vell said. "I have made such magnificent progress!"

"And you've destroyed so much!" Even said. "What about the stability of the borderlands? The lake that moved? The hill? And what if that instability spreads? The unicorns said it could. It could affect all of Firoth!"

Waving her hand as if this was of no concern, Lady Vell said dismissively, "I'll research a solution, when I have the time." From her tone, Even knew she'd do no such thing.

"I have the solution right here." Even lifted the soda can.

"Wait! Don't you want to have magic all the time?" Lady Vell said. "Don't you want to be able to do extraordinary things?"

Why doesn't she use her magic on me? Even wondered. *Why try to convince me to stop?* Lady Vell could just walk through her own barrier and . . .

She can't.

However Lady Vell had made the last bubble of protection, it was built to stop *all* magic, which meant even Lady Vell, full of her stolen magic, couldn't cross it. Here and now, being magic-less was its own kind of magic.

"You and I, we're not so different," Lady Vell said. "I too was born without magic. Yet I yearned for more. You yearn for more too. I know what you want, in your heart of hearts."

"You don't," Even said. "You don't know me at all. Sure, having magic every day would be great, but it's not the most important thing to me. You don't know what's important to me. You never asked. You never cared—you never cared what anyone else wanted, but what other people want matters too." She shook the can one more time, and then she opened it. "And I want my family back."

The spray rocketed out, landing on the power stone. The

lightning fizzled. Even emptied the rest of the can onto the stone, shaking it until every drop dribbled out.

"No!" Lady Vell cried.

The sparks from the stone sputtered—and then stopped.

Across the workroom, the vat of stolen magic began to rumble.

20

THROUGHOUT THE TOWER, the vines began to droop as the magic receded. Blue sparks fizzled as power drained from the leaves.

"Freedom!" Jeremy shouted as he broke out of the greenery with a majestic leap.

"Find Odd!" Even called to him. "Check the solarium!" He raced for the other room as she sprinted across the lab, leaping over the vines as they writhed and fell to the ground. She couldn't let Lady Vell catch her.

"What have you done?" Lady Vell howled, and Even felt herself lifted up into the air by the back of her shirt. She flailed her arms and legs in the air, trying to resist.

But it was an odd day. She had no magic to fight Lady Vell. *It won't last,* Even thought. Lady Vell's magic was stolen. Just like the vines' power had been. And as with the vines, hers would fade too. But would it fade fast enough? Even was pulled back like a fish on a reel.

From the solarium, Jeremy cried, "Found her!"

Then he burst into the room, with Odd on his back.

"Odd, skunk me!" Even yelled as she felt Lady Vell's hand close around her wrist. Her fingers were bony, and she squeezed so tight that it hurt.

Odd squinched up her face, concentrating, and Even's body began to tingle. Fur sprouted on her skin. Still held in the air by Lady Vell's magic, she shrank quickly. She felt her hands curl into paws, and Lady Vell lost her grip on Even's wrist.

Lifting up her gloriously fluffy tail, Even sprayed, aiming at Lady Vell's face.

Coughing, Lady Vell lost her magical grip on her as well, and Even tumbled to the floor. She landed on a floating board —Jeremy had shoved it across the workroom just in time. She rode it toward her sister as Lady Vell regained herself.

"Do you know what you did?" Lady Vell raged.

"Yeah, we stopped you from destroying families and homes," Odd said as Even reached her. Odd put her hand on Even's furry back, and they faced Lady Vell together. "We stopped you from stealing what other people need."

"And we did it without magic," Even said. "Well, except the skunk thing."

Odd shot her a smile, and Even curled her skunk's mouth up to smile back at her.

"Shortsighted, selfish, stupid children! You destroyed my life's work. I have devoted my life to discoveries that would benefit—"

"Other people have lives too!" Even cut her off. "Hopes, dreams, homes. Those matter too, and you treated them as disposable. It doesn't matter why you think you did it—it was wrong. The way to help people isn't to hurt them!"

Behind Lady Vell, Even saw that the vat of blue bubbles was evaporating away, as the liquid dispersed into a blue cloud and rose up toward the light at the top of the tower. "And now you won't be able to hurt anyone anymore," Even said. "See for yourself."

"Oh no, you're not distracting me," Lady Vell said. "My magic—"

"'Your' magic is going back where it belongs," a new voice said.

"Mom!" Even and Odd cried. She was okay!

As Lady Vell turned, Even and Odd saw that Mom wasn't alone. Everyone who had accompanied her on her official quest was here. Like Jeremy, they'd been trapped in the vines. And like him, they'd been released when the magic began to fail. They advanced on Lady Vell.

A man with a single eye pushed aside the now-motionless

creepy dolls, while the unicorns leveled their horns menacingly at Lady Vell. One wizard held a purple fireball in her hands. She tossed it back and forth, and it grew.

"The dam is broken," Mom said to Lady Vell. "You don't have access to a reservoir of stolen magic anymore, Vell. Soon, it will all return to its source. Now . . . *step away from my children.*" She marched forward.

The wizard sent her fireball spinning across the room, and the flames wrapped around Lady Vell's wrists like handcuffs. As the centaur guard charged at the wizard, she shot another fireball, handcuffing his hands and hooves in flames as well.

Even, Odd, and Jeremy let out cheers.

Glaring at them, Lady Vell struggled against the fire cuffs, but they held her and the centaur tight as the last of the blue liquid dissipated.

Jeremy's parents trotted over to Jeremy. "Did she hurt you?" Starry asked. "Are you okay?" She prodded him gently with her horn, as if checking for injuries.

"Mom! Dad! So great to see you!" Jeremy said to them. "I don't even care if you punish me again for borrowing the invisibility cloak and kind of letting it get destroyed."

"I think saving your parents earns you forgiveness," his mother said. She nuzzled his face with hers. Their horns clinked together with a sound like champagne flutes. "Wait, you destroyed Uncle Sunflower's cloak?"

"It never fit him anyway," his father said. "You're forgiven."

Mom hurried toward Even and Odd, stepping over the wilted vines, the limp dolls, and the scattered boards. "Are you two all right? Odd, did you skunk your sister again?"

"I asked her to," Even said.

Starry stepped forward and declared in a ringing voice, "We will send word to the Academy of Magic about what transpired here. I believe they will be *very* interested in Lady Vell's recent activities. I can guarantee that after this, she will not be allowed to cause any more trouble."

Effervescent Spring added, "You can be certain we unicorns will be keeping a close eye on her. In fact, I think the whole world will."

Picking up Even by her furry stomach, Mom wrapped her arms around Odd. Even was squished between them, but it was a nice squish. She made a skunk purring sound. "Can we go home now?" Even asked.

★★★

Lady Vell was taken, along with her centaur guard, by some of Mom's allies to be transported directly to the Academy of Magic headquarters, east of the dragon territories. Even, Odd, and Mom watched them load her and her vat onto a cart pulled by four winged horses.

"She didn't think it mattered that she was hurting people,"

Even said. Lady Vell had claimed she was helping people, but instead she'd caused pain and chaos.

"Lady Vell won't hurt anyone again," Mom said.

"We will spread the truth of what happened here to all," Starry promised.

Together, they all watched the flying cart with Lady Vell disappear into the clouds.

After it was gone, Mom herded Even and Odd back into the city, to the house with the purple Seuss tress, while Jeremy and his parents went to find the rabbit reporter. The evening felt so strangely quiet after everything that had happened. Even the city itself seemed subdued.

It fit Even's mood.

She'd always wanted to be a hero, to have her own quest, to do something that was important, but she'd always thought of that as something she'd do in the distant future, when she felt ready. *I never felt ready for this,* she thought. She'd been scared a lot, worried a lot, and uncertain a lot. None of it had felt the way she'd imagined a quest would feel, but she'd done it anyway. Maybe "ready" didn't matter as much as she'd thought it did. Maybe what mattered was that you did it anyway.

Even, Odd, and Mom went inside their old house, and Mom transformed Even back into her human self. "Thanks, Mom!" Even stretched her neck and her arms, shaking out the last of the tingles. "You know, I kind of like being a skunk. There are pluses."

"And definite minuses," Odd said, wrinkling her nose.

Mom waved her hand, and the scent of flowers wafted through the room. And in that instant, Even realized that it was over. Lady Vell had been stopped, the border magic had (hopefully) returned, and both worlds should be back to normal, or on their way to normal.

"It's over," Even said, letting the words roll around inside her. It didn't feel real. And yet . . . she knew what she'd seen and heard and felt and done, even if she didn't yet know what she thought about all of it.

The three of them stared at one another. And then they burst out talking all at once. "You did it!" "We did it!" "How did you—" "Are you okay?" "You could have been—" "But we weren't!" "I didn't think—" "What if she—" "Did we really do it?" "Is everything fixed?" "Can we go home?"

They paused, looked at one another again, and started laughing so hard they couldn't speak. Even didn't know why she was laughing, since none of this was funny, but it felt right. A tear slid down her cheek, and she wiped it with the back of her hand. Odd's eyes were wet too.

Eventually, they all calmed down.

Jeremy and his parents returned a little while later, and Mom insisted on feeding everyone and shooing them to their beds to sleep. She'd call Dad and tell him they were all okay, she promised. As eager as they all were to be home, it was a half-day journey to Lakeview and a few hours more to the gateway that would take them back to Stony Haven, so they should rest and recover first. They'd be home tomorrow.

Even had said that so many times over the past few days —*we'll be home tomorrow*—but this time, finally, she believed it.

★★★

In the morning, Even and Odd helped their mother close up the house, while Jeremy and his parents went out to buy food for their journey. The sisters unhooked the hammocks and stuffed them into bags, they cleaned up the dishes their guests had used, and they shut all the windows. Once they finished, they stepped outside so Mom could shrink their home into the size of a brick. After carefully marking it with their name, she took them to a wall of tiny doors and placed their home in what looked like a post-office box. She sealed it in with a lock.

It felt so final. Even felt the weight of everything she could have had but had given up. Daily magic. Maybe even a future here.

"Will we ever come back?" she asked.

Mom put her arm around her. Side by side, they regarded the wall that held their shrunken home. "How about we make my next business trip into a family trip?"

"Really?" Even asked.

"Yes, really."

Odd jumped in. "But it won't be *too* soon, right? I haven't been to the animal shelter in days, and I know the dogs must miss me. Plus there are supposed to be new kittens."

Even knew that wasn't the real reason, or at least not the only reason, that Odd didn't want to come back too soon: she wanted to be safe and sound at home for a while before venturing back into Firoth. Even didn't blame her.

"It won't be too soon," Mom promised. "Come on, girls. Your father is waiting for us."

They met up with Jeremy and his parents on the street that cut through the city. Each unicorn carried a satchel with breakfast and lunch.

Jeremy asked Even and Odd, "Ready to go home?"

"Seriously? You have to ask?" Odd said. "Obviously."

"How about you?" Even asked.

"I just want to see with my own eyes that home is where it's supposed to be."

With Odd riding Jeremy, Even on Starry, and Mom on Effervescent Spring, they joined a stream of travelers heading from the capital out to the borderlands. Even wondered if Lady Vell understood how many people her actions had affected. Would she care if she knew? Was there a point when she would have started caring?

I cared, Even thought. *And so did Odd and Jeremy.*

In the end, that had turned out to be enough.

Everyone on the yellow brick road was smiling and joking. Some were singing. It felt like being in a parade, especially with so many creatures—winged horses, eagles with human heads, a snake with bat wings—floating above the road like balloons.

Beneath the joy, though, all of them had the same worries: Would the gateways be open? Would they be able to go home and have home be the same as they remembered? Would they see their families again?

As they drew closer to the borderlands, Even saw the scars from the chaos that Lady Vell had caused. The yellow brick road was torn up, with crevasses that split it like wounds. Makeshift bridges had been built across the gaps, using uprooted trees and boards from collapsed houses. One house was crushed in a crater shaped like a giant footprint.

Clusters of tents had been set up as emergency clinics, and Even saw an array of flower fairies lying on cots, being tended to by a large spider who was using his legs to wrap petals in bandages. Mom jogged over to talk with the spider and then returned. "A hydra appeared away from its territory. It's gone now, but it caught a flock of fairies by surprise."

Continuing on, they saw other evidence of disruption to the

lives of those who lived along the border: trampled fields, fallen trees, scorched farmland, collapsed houses. But already there were signs of rebuilding: using tools and magic, people were fixing houses, repairing fields, and hauling trees off roads.

With time, things would get back to normal.

And that, Even told herself, was a good thing.

★★★

As they approached Lakeview, Even could tell that Jeremy was getting nervous. They couldn't see yet if Lakeview had its lake or the unicorns' hill. She and Odd walked next to him. "I'll replace your soda," she said, hoping to distract him from worrying.

"And we can play Farmcats," Odd said, "next time you visit."

Jeremy shot a look at his parents.

"You already confessed," Odd reminded him. "It's a little late to worry about them overhearing."

"I'm hoping they'll forget I disobeyed them," Jeremy said.

Even grinned. "It's fun to be an optimist."

As they drew closer, she heard shrieking. Many voices, very high and off-pitch, wailed in piercing dissonance. But she smiled as she clapped her hands over her ears. Hearing mermaids— that was an excellent sign.

Entering the town, they saw the lake: the very same lake they'd seen before, but back in its proper location. A few mermaids were splashing happily in the shallows.

Joj the goblin waved at them from near the shore. "Got my lake back!"

"Congratulations," Odd said.

He pointed at a squat brick house that was shaped like a beehive. "And my house. See?"

"And the mermaids?" Even asked, even though she could hear them. "Are they all okay?"

"It was a close call," Joj said. "But they're back where they belong, and the salmon are running in the river. Everything's okay. I . . . I am sorry I had to leave."

He'd done what he'd thought was best. They all had. "I'm glad you're back where you want to be," Even said.

Watching the mermaids play in the lake, she smiled as they shrieked to one another. *We really did it,* Even thought. *We fixed things.* She hadn't needed any special wizard medallion or training to be a hero. She hadn't had to wait until she was eighteen. She'd been able to make a difference as she was, right now.

"Wait here." Joj disappeared into his beehive house and re-emerged with a basket piled high with pastries and fruits. He shoved it at Mom and mumbled, "As thanks for all your family did."

"Thank you," Mom said. "We can repay you—"

"Already paid in full," Joj said. "Now scat. It's your turn to find your home."

***

It was evening by the time they reached the unicorns' hill in its proper location. Whinnying in delight, Jeremy raced up the slope. He frolicked in the blanket of flowers, and the other unicorns reared back and then laughed.

Coming up the slope on foot, Even, Odd, and Mom were welcomed by the entire herd. "Consider yourself part of our family," Starry Delight told them. "Visit anytime."

"Thank you," Mom said. "You are always welcome to visit us as well."

And then it was time to go home.

Odd took the lead at a run, and Even and Mom chased after her. The first stars were beginning to appear as they hurried back to the yellow brick road and around Unicorn Hill, toward the wall of mist that marked the border.

Even saw the gateway first: golden and glowing in the murky whiteness.

She slowed and looked back at the world around her, enveloped in evening shadows. The grass and flowers in the meadow were gray in the dusk, but it was all still so beautiful. "I'll come back," she whispered aloud.

Odd shouted, "Mom! It's here!"

"Hold hands," Mom instructed. She held out both her hands. Even took one and Odd the other. They didn't hesitate. Together, they walked between worlds.

***

They emerged in the employee parking lot behind the bagel store. Even immediately smelled the warm sweetness of just-baked bagels, the hint of car exhaust, and the sickly stench of the dumpster. Happily, it didn't smell quite as ripe as it had when she'd worn a skunk's nose.

"Home!" Odd cried.

Rushing to the back door of the bagel shop, Even flung it open. Light flooded into the parking lot. "Mr. Fratelli? It's Even Berry. Are you baking?"

"Hello, my dear!" a voice floated back. "It's a miracle! The gateway is back! I got word from my daughter—all is well!"

Inside, Even saw bagel dough twisting itself into circles in midair and powdered sugar falling like snow. With a cheerful smile on his face, Mr. Fratelli bustled toward them. He kissed Mom on each cheek and then pressed a bag of bagels into her arms. "French toast for your girls!" he said.

"Thank you, Mr. Fratelli," Mom said. "Glad to see you back in business."

He patted Even on the head. "You, my dear, look much better as yourself than as a skunk."

"You saw?" Even asked. "You knew?"

"I saw you on the shop's surveillance cameras. You were so brave, going through the gateway! Do you know why our magic left and why it came back? Is it here to stay?"

"We believe it is," Mom said.

A familiar but less-welcome voice said, "As soon as my order is complete, I will be underway, never to return." The elf priestess rose from her seat beyond the counter. She still wore her ornate robe, but her pink hair had unraveled from its many jewels. A few of the flowers in her hair had wilted.

"I'd thought you'd be in a hurry to get home," Even said. "Doesn't your daughter have her ceremony?"

"I have missed it already," the elf said stiffly. "Just as you have missed your exam."

That stung, of course, but Even wasn't going to let the elf priestess see that. "There are some things that matter more."

Mom laid her hand on Even's shoulder. "We are going to appeal to the Academy of Magic for an alternate date, since they were in no position to administer the test on the required day."

The elf sniffed in obvious disapproval, but Even didn't care. She smiled at her mother. Mom thought she was ready. That mattered a lot more than the opinion of a snooty elf priestess.

"Safe travels," Mom told the elf. They thanked Mr. Fratelli for the bagels, and Mom drove them home. Leaning against the car window, Even looked out at their normal, familiar town, without a single mermaid, hydra, or flower fairy, and was happy to be back.

Mom pulled into their driveway. All the lights were on, as

were the lights in the fairies' house. They rushed out of the car and toward the shop.

"Dad!" they shouted.

He burst outside, his arms wide, his hair wild, as if he hadn't washed or brushed it in days, and his smile was so big that he looked as if he was about to cry. Even and Odd ran into his arms at the same time. Mom came up behind them and plopped a kiss on Dad's lips.

"Is everything back to normal here?" Mom asked.

"Everything is perfect, now that you're all back," Dad said. "I was beyond worried." He hugged them tighter, and a few tears leaked out of the corners of his eyes.

"We're sorry, Dad," Odd said.

"I'm sorry," Even said. "It was my fault."

"It was both our faults," Odd said. "We went together." She squeezed Even's hand.

Mom stepped in. "And they saved the day together. Even and Odd discovered the cause of all the problems with the border, and they were the ones who resolved it. Come on, let's go in. We have a lot to tell you!"

They went inside, through the shop, and into the kitchen. Dad had cleaned the pancake batter from the counter and floor, but there was an open box of Lucky Charms cereal on the table, empty, and no sign that Dad had been eating anything else while they were gone. *He's really been worried,* Even thought. Dad usually loved to cook and eat. He happily took the bag of bagels from Mom.

"French-toast-bagel dessert?" Even suggested.

"Sounds magical," Odd said.

Even grinned at her, and Odd grinned back.

Using her magic, Even flew the bagels out of their bag, while Odd, by hand, set plates on the table. Dad fetched cream cheese and jelly from the fridge. Mom made calls, letting neighbors know that the gateway was operational and would stay that way—the Academy of Magic was watching now. Also the unicorns.

Lots of people will be watching, Even thought.

If enough people and creatures stayed alert and didn't just rely on the Academy or a hero or someone else to do the right thing, then the border would never close again. Even could have both worlds.

Two homes, she thought as she spread cream cheese on her bagel.

Two homes and one family.

She liked the sound of that.

Laughing together, they told stories about their adventures late into the night.

★★★

The next day, an odd day, Even woke in her own bed, and for the first time ever, she didn't mind so much not having magic. After all, she had defeated Lady Vell on a magicless day. She knew she'd remember that moment for the rest of her life, no matter what kind of day it was.

She sat up.

Without warning, she felt her skin tingle and fur sprout. Glancing across the room, she saw Odd already awake and, to Even's surprise, floating a few feet above her bed. Odd's forehead was crinkled in concentration. Even felt a skunk tail unfurl from her rear. She waved it delightedly in the air. "You're practicing!" Even said.

"Thought I should start doing that more."

"You . . . don't mind still having magic? And still sharing magic? I had to choose. For both of us. I'm sorry—there wasn't time to ask you."

"I know," Odd said as she sank onto her pillow. "Look, I still don't *like* having to worry about my magic bursting out at the wrong moment, but it's worth it to have helped all those families." She grinned. "And it's not so terrible to have to practice."

Even grinned back.

"Right now I'm going to practice turning you into yourself again."

"That's all right," Even said, hopping down from the bed.

She twisted, examining her fur from all angles. "I kind of think it suits me, at least once in a while."

Odd's grin turned sly. "Does this mean you've decided you'd rather be a talking-animal sidekick than a hero?"

"It means I'm already a hero," Even said. "*And* a talking-animal sidekick." She trotted out of the room with her tail held high. "How about breakfast? I'm in the mood for pancakes."

ACKNOWLEDGMENTS

Every night, I used to check the back of my closet for a doorway to a magic world. Every birthday, I'd wish for a magic wand. Every summer, I'd search the woods behind our house for a dragon's egg or a stray unicorn. But I never found one.

When I was ten years old, I decided that if I couldn't *find* magic, then I'd simply have to *make* it.

I started to write.

Even and Odd is my twenty-third book. It's inspired by a childhood spent searching for wizards and unicorns. When I sat down to write *Even and Odd*, I had one goal in mind: write a story filled with as much magic as I could pour into it. It's for anyone who has ever checked the back of their closet for a portal, picked up a stick and pretended it was a wand, or imagined what it would be like to walk on four paws.

And it wouldn't exist without a whole slew of magical people behind it. Thank you to my phenomenal editor, Anne Hoppe, and my amazing agent, Andrea Somberg, as well as Amanda

Acevedo, Lisa DiSarro, Candice Finn, Eleanor Hinkle, Catherine Onder, Sharismar Rodriguez, Opal Roengchai, Jackie Sassa, Helen Seachrist, John Sellers, Tara Shanahan, Karen Sherman, Dinah Stevenson, Kaitlin Yang, and all the other awesome people at Clarion Books and Houghton Mifflin Harcourt for bringing this story to life! And a special thank you to the incredible Brandon Dorman for the fantastic cover art!

Much love and many thanks to my husband, my children, and all my family and friends. You add magic to my life—and to the world—every day.

ABOUT THE AUTHOR

Sarah Beth Durst has written fantasy novels for readers of all ages. Her books for children include *Spark, Catalyst, The Stone Girl's Story,* and *The Girl Who Could Not Dream,* which was named a best book of the year by *Kirkus Reviews.* A three-time finalist for the Andre Norton Award for YA Science Fiction and Fantasy, Sarah has won the Mythopoeic Fantasy Award for Children's Literature and an American Library Association Alex Award, which is given to books written for adults that hold special appeal to young adults.

Sarah Beth Durst lives with her family and mischievous cat in Stony Brook, New York.

sarahbethdurst.com

Twitter and Instagram: @sarahbethdurst